The Sad Kitchen

© 2020 **John Paul King**

Galaxy Galloper Press

Cover Art by John Paul King

ISBN:9781733233200

Published by Galaxy Galloper Press, LLC

galaxygalloper@gmail.com

John Paul King

THE SAD KITCHEN

For Hannah

The Sad Kitchen

JOHN PAUL KING

CHAPTER ONE

The Sad Kitchen is a friendly place. It is a diner where people who are sad come in the nighttime, and I am their waiter. Back in the kitchen my wife does the cooking and makes the tickets. She's the angel of this operation. Helen. We serve only breakfast at the Sad Kitchen and are open all night.

Tonight, Vern is here. Vern is a frequenter of the Sad Kitchen. Vern was in prison once, but they let him go very early in his sentence because a tree grew up through the cement floor of his prison cell (he tells me), a tree which was so strong the guards couldn't chop it down. They tried to take it down with a chainsaw, but the chainsaw was only a back-scratch for the tree. You could practically see the tree smiling when they put the chainsaw to it, claimed Vern.

The parole board thought the miraculous occurrence of the tree in the prison cell meant Vern was an innocent man even though he told them in no uncertain terms that that wasn't true. He was guilty of it. But they gave him early parole anyway, and very quietly. The story was kept quiet to avoid humiliating the justice system, Vern claimed. Now Vern comes to the Sad Kitchen with much frequency. It's a very strange story, but he sure sticks to it.

In all other aspects of conversation, I've found Vern to be a serious and levelheaded fellow. "Plate of eggs and potatoes and something for the children," was Vern's order tonight. "And some coffee, sad."

So I went back and got Vern's plate and his ticket from my wife. Helen was delighted to give him something for the children. Her joy was made apparent to me by the way she stopped what she was doing and put the back of her hand on her hip.

After a little bit of gentle contemplation, my wife scribbled on a greasy ticket and handed it over so I could deliver it to Vern. Vern's ticket had something to do with writing a children's book about the tree in his prison cell that could make a little child smile.

"This is a tough one, Bubba," said Vern, folding the ticket and putting it in the breast pocket of his tired, old flannel shirt at two in the morning, which is the time he normally comes to the Sad Kitchen. The Sad Kitchen is busiest at the hours when people wake up and can't go back to sleep. "A good one but sure a tough one," said Vern taking his first sip of coffee.

After Vern finished his meal, he stepped out into the dark street but came back a few minutes later. "Bubba?" he said.

"Yeah, Vern?"

"Is the story supposed to make the little child smile in the book, or is the book supposed to make some other little child smile—some child not in the book."

"Might be either, Vern. Might be you could make it a book that makes a little child smile in the book, and it will make a little child smile not in the book, too."

There was a nervous or overwhelmed look in his eye.

"Say Vern, I can go ask my wife if you would like some clarification."

"That's okay," he said in a very definite way that made me fear he still didn't quite understand. "Tell Helen I am grateful," Vern said and headed out.

Helen used to visit folks in prison. That was how we met. I was a prisoner in the ward she used to visit. I was released from prison not because of a tree growing up through the floor of my cell, but for the normal reason people are released from prison.

When folks used to ask what I was in prison for, I would say, "THE unspeakable crime." Those were back in the days when I had a little more energy to devote to being a jokester.

The Sad Kitchen is a gentle place. Around 3 a.m. Mike with Tourettes comes in yammering. At the counter he flails his limbs as I fill his coffee cup, sad, and he yammers on and on. "I socked her," he says. "I got her with a quick jab and then I put my knee to her gut. Then I took

12

her by the throat. And all of this was right in front of my little daughter." On and on like that goes Mike. He's done this for five years now, the same spiel. My wife has explained to him that it's not necessary, but he insists. Each night he does it.

Then he grows quiet, hunches over his coffee cup as if to let the steam warm his face.

"What's my ticket tonight, Bubba?" asks Mike after his ritual.

Karen comes in before work, around 5 a.m. She's a lawyer in one of the skyscrapers. I don't know why Karen comes to the Sad Kitchen. It is difficult for me to imagine the reason folks with jobs in skyscrapers would come to a place like this. My wife encourages me not to spend too much time speculating on it. Helen always says remorse feels exactly the same regardless of what caused it. Helen also always says that the tricky part about the phrase *What Would Jesus Do?* is that the most difficult time to do what Jesus would do is after you've already done something He would NEVER do. But it's also the most critical moment, she says. And the idea behind the tickets at the Sad Kitchen, says my wife, is to help folks with this very critical moment. Sometimes this critical moment can last many years.

I've asked Karen (and some of the other skyscraper customers—we have a few accountants and a banker) what the city looks like from way up high. "It looks sad, Bubba," they tell me. "You would never know that anything is getting accomplished up there or that any sort of progress is being made because, day in and day out, the view is always the same and it never changes. You can stand at the window and watch the world become part of the sky, and it never changes."

Valli with the underbite comes in at unpredictable times. Often she arrives drunk or worse at the Sad Kitchen. She lives on the streets of downtown, and the streets of downtown have become her.

If I wasn't careful when I looked at Valli the only thing I saw was a gray downtown street corner set against a huge gray building under a low gray sky, and the wind whips across the sidewalk with grates out of which steam rises and swirls into nothingness, like a ghost of all the people who walk past Valli, bundled up around her paper cup.

Helen still serves Valli when she is drunk or worse. Valli hardly eats anything anyway. She just wants some sad coffee and her ticket and the warmth.

Valli looks to be about 45 years of age, and I would therefore estimate her to be approximately 30 years of age. Valli has approximately as many strands of hair as most people have teeth, and approximately as many teeth as a newborn baby.

By 6:30 a.m. each morning we get a few final Sad Kitchen customers mixed in with *real* customers, along with a fellow named Jack.

What I mean by "real" is folks who aren't customers of the Sad Kitchen, but are actually customers of Jack's Diner.

Jack's Diner is the Sad Kitchen during the daytime, and Jack's Diner has paying customers all throughout the day until 7 p.m. when the alley outside grows dark and lonely and grim, like the last place on earth a flower would grow or a unicorn would make its existence known to mankind. Instead of a flower or a unicorn, Helen comes and the Sad Kitchen is open again for another night.

15

Jack's Diner is in the phone book and has a mailing address and some revenue.

The owner of Jack's Diner is an old friend of Helen's, Jack. Jack is the father of Helen's dead son, although Jack and Helen were never married, and that is something Helen has come to terms with. Jack lends Helen the space and is also a proud customer of the Sad Kitchen.

The day's seventh hour is the only hour where Jack's Diner customers and Sad Kitchen customers overlap. It is during the day's seventh hour that Jack himself goes from being a customer of the Sad Kitchen to being the owner of his own operation: Jack's Diner.

If Helen is the angel of this operation (which she is), then Jack is the providing father.

It is quite a dramatic and abrupt shift for Jack, but he handles it modestly. At the bottom of the day's sixth hour he is sitting at the counter of the Sad Kitchen searching for answers in his coffee, sad, and by the top of the next hour he is writing the day's special on a chalkboard. Lasagna, potpie, chili, alfredo, these sorts of things. His ticket is perpetually the same: *Lend us your kitchen, dear friend!* And he always does.

We never ask folks to explain their presence at the Sad Kitchen.

Folks hear about the Sad Kitchen and they come.

The Sad Kitchen is not a secret operation, but it is funny the things that remain secretive because folks are looking elsewhere.

If it is the day's seventh hour, I face the task of determining whether a customer needs a normal Jack's Diner ticket or a special Sad Kitchen ticket. If they need a Sad Kitchen ticket, they say, "What's my ticket?" with sadness in their eyes. Really the art of determining which ticket a customer needs is no art at all. I know the face of remorse like an old friend.

It was midnight the following night when Vern entered with his book—just a messy bundle of papers. Valli with the underbite sat at the end of the counter and brought her coffee mug to her bottom lip with a blunted sense of astonishment, as if the cup were a chalice that she didn't quite understand.

"Kind of early to be seeing you, Vern, isn't it?" I said as I poured him some coffee, sad.

"I've been up all day and night working on this little book," said Vern. "I didn't even bother to try to sleep tonight. I was too worked up. Say, Bubba, I want Helen to read it."

I went through the bat-wing doors into the back to grab my wife, who was in the midst of cracking eggs for a long night.

Helen came out and read Vern's mess of papers and, on the final page, a tear sprouted from her eye. With this, Vern also grew misty. "Well, shoot. It was supposed to make a little child smile, not make an old lady cry!"

We have moments like this at the Sad Kitchen from time to time. Now a tear dripped from my chin. I am never aware that I am crying until a tear drips from my chin.

"I want to see!" blurted Valli now from her place at the end of the counter.

So Helen brought the book over to Valli and said, "Here you go, Sweetie."

Valli took the bundle of papers and it was as if she were taking a newborn child. She had no clue what to do with it, but she knew that it was magnificent. She started getting the pages all mixed around and Vern stood from his seat, "Wait, that's not—"

But Helen held up her hand to shush Vern and said to Valli, "Hey Valli, how about Vern reads his book to you?"

I guess my wife had deduced something that Vern and I had overlooked: Valli didn't know how to read.

"That's something I'd be proud to do, Miss Helen," said Vern.

So Vern and Valli went into a booth and Vern read his book to Valli and sure enough after a few minutes Valli was not crying, but giggling.

My wife looked on like a proud mother.

I have heard Valli laugh before. She has a very deranged laugh that could wilt a flower on the spot. But this laugh was different as she listened to Vern's book. This laugh was just a giggle, just a teacup filled with her childhood.

19

That night brought a normal flow of customers to the Sad Kitchen. My wife was feeling generous and especially touched by Vern's book, so she made all the tickets easy: *Sit and listen to Vern's book*.

Fireman John Rogers, whom I've never heard utter a single word, came in around one in the morning, his usual time, and, with his usual stone-faced, public officer's scowl, listened to Vern's reading.

But afterward, Fireman John Rogers came back up to the counter, very shy, and spoke the first words I have ever heard him speak. "May I speak to Miss Helen?"

I grabbed my wife and they went over to a corner where nobody could hear their conversation. John Rogers was sheepish about whatever he wanted to discuss with my wife. I watched them out of the sharpest corner of my eye while I served the other customers. Afterward, my wife told me what Fireman John Rogers had discussed with her: he wanted a copy of Vern's book so he could bring it home and read it to his little daughter.

And Fireman John Rogers wasn't the only one to request a copy, either. Mike with Tourettes had the same request, although he was less discrete about it. Mike is discrete about nothing. "I need me a copy of that! I'll read it to my little girl!"

We had about six or seven more requests that night. Folks were very interested.

During a quiet period around five in the morning, Vern read his book to me. He was just sitting in the booth with nobody to read to, so I said, "Hey, Vern, I haven't heard the story yet."

So he came up to the counter and read it to me. It was five in the morning at the Sad Kitchen and there is nothing else for me to report, so I will take this opportunity to mention briefly what Vern's story is about. I will try to do a good job, but I fear I will lack Vern's magic touch. Nevertheless, here goes:

The story begins when a young bunny rabbit named Vernon was hopping along the grass with his mother and they came across a lovely sunflower in a garden. Vernon, the young rabbit, wanted to pick the sunflower and bring it home into their rabbit hole, but his mother, very stern, told him "No, Vernon," because the sunflower belonged in Miss Johnson's garden, and it was Miss Johnson's sunflower, and if Vernon took the flower with him then nobody else would get to see how lovely it was. Vern pouted and pouted all the way home.

Well that day while Vernon's mother was busy cleaning the rabbit hole, Vernon snuck out and plucked Miss Johnson's sunflower and brought it home—a very sneaky little rabbit. But, as these things always seem to go for us thieves, when Vern's mother was cleaning the rabbit hole later that day, she found a lonely yellow petal on the floor and knew right away what Vernon had done. She came into Vernon's bedroom and, sure enough, little Vernon was in the middle of hiding Miss Johnson's sunflower in his bedroom. So Vernon was sent to timeout in the darkest part of his mother's office in the coldest nook of the rabbit hole.

This next part is where I stopped wiping the counter and was all ears as Vern (the human) read his story. While little Vernon (the bunny) was shivering-cold and lonely in his timeout, a tree suddenly sprouted from below and carried Vernon out of timeout and through the ground and into the sky. Now he was all of a sudden among the tree's highest branches and was warm in the sunshine and felt very free: ecstasy for little Vernon!

Little Vernon started hopping around and swinging from branch to branch—a very happy rabbit.

But by and by something sad occurred. From up in the tree, Vernon could see Miss Johnson mosey across the lawn and into her garden. Her flower was gone. Vernon had a perfect view of her sad face. There was nothing he could do but watch Miss Johnson's sadness become itself.

Vernon suddenly felt very alone and very scared up in the tree. He realized that he didn't know how to climb trees, so he wasn't sure how he would get down. Plus, he noticed a hungry hawk with a narrow eye beginning to swoop past the tree, closer and closer to Vernon's branch. Vernon's mother had warned him about hawks.

Vernon wanted to call for his mother, but if he shouted her name, the hungry hawk might hear his shouts.

Vernon was about to start crying when, out of nowhere, a lovely dove came and landed on Vernon's branch. "Are you a friendly dove?" asked the scared little rabbit. But the dove didn't answer, just came and put a wing around Vernon's shoulder.

"I did something very bad," said Vernon,

trembling under the dove's wing, "and now I'm scared."

The dove held Vernon closer in his wings—very precious.

"What am I going to do?" cried Vernon. "I ruined Miss Johnson's lovely sunflower and now I'm stuck up in this tree when I'm supposed to be in timeout. And there is a hungry hawk flying around out there!"

"Hop on my back and I will bring you safely back to your mother," said the dove.

Vernon was very grateful for the dove's kindness. But one thing was still bothering him. "I don't know how I can face my mother after what I did to Miss Johnson's sunflower."

"I know what you can do," said the nice dove, very elegant.

The dove returned Vernon to the ground and Vernon invited the dove into the rabbit hole and introduced the dove to his mother.

Of course, Vernon's mother was suspicious ("Aren't you supposed to be in timeout, young man?") but she was impressed by Vernon's new friend, the dove, who had good manners. Together, Vernon and his friend the dove told Vernon's mother the plan.

The dove taught Vernon and his mother how to find seeds in the eye of the sunflower that Vernon had plucked from Miss Johnson's garden, and together they went out into Miss Johnson's garden and planted some seeds. The story ends on a page with no words, just a lousy but wholesome drawing of three new sunflowers in Miss Johnson's garden, and the dove is flying into the sun.

I can see I've failed. I told the story as truly as I could, but there was more to Vern's story than just the story itself.

There were the drawings, of course, (lousy but wholesome) but there was more than that too.

The truth is: it is impossible to tell a children's story in the middle of a story that is otherwise so distant from childhood.

The truth is: the reason Vern (the person, not the rabbit) was in prison was that he raped a young girl about eight years ago when he was working as a plumber. The little girl's name was Izzy, and she bore a little son as a result of the attack. Eight years later, Vern has never met the son. Vern has spent the rest of his life, these eight years, trying to figure out whether the concept of forgiveness is too good to be true. "What's the catch?" he has asked my wife many nights at the Sad Kitchen, his voice and his posture absolutely crushed by the aggregate of eight years' remorse.

Helen takes him into the corner booth and talks to him about how the Holy Spirit is at work in him, and usually they are able to sort through all that strangling, suffocating guilt until, together, they find what they are looking for: the love of the Holy Spirit at work in Vern. And Helen gives him his ticket for the night.

That night, Vern left his book with my wife so she could make a few copies. On the drive home that morning I said to Helen, "Well I guess we better make a few copies of Vern's book."

Helen laughed and agreed. It had been so well received by folks. We went to a print shop near our home and Helen went inside to make some copies while I took a nap in the car. I'm always dog-tired after my Sad Kitchen shifts.

Helen came back into the car and I woke up.

"Where are the copies?" I asked her. "Are you looking for someone with a strong back and a weak mind to haul them out here?"

"They said they would bind them for me and we can pick them up this evening, isn't that nice? I ordered fifty copies."

"Fifty!"

"It's a special book, Bubba."

That evening we stopped by the print shop on the way back downtown, and during that night's shift we passed out 12 copies of Vern's book. A few folks asked Vern to sign the book—just as a joke. At first Vern was endorsing his small fame, albeit in a very modest and pleasant way.

"Man Vern!" yelled Mike with Tourettes while Vern signed his copy. "You've got one helluva imagination!"

It got to where Vern didn't know what to say. "Shoot," he'd say and sign the book and look away, sheepish.

"You okay Vern?" I asked during a rare moment of peace that night as I filled his coffee, sad, and noticed Vern's downcast eyes.

"Hey, Bubba, can you grab Miss Helen a moment?" said Vern, nervous.

I went through the bat-wing doors and fetched my wife, who was standing over the industrial-sized skillet dealing with some hash browns.

"Hi, Sweetie," said Helen to Vern. "Everything okay?"

Quiet, Vern said, "Folks all think I used my imagination to make that book. But really it happened just the way I told it."

"I believe you," said Helen, patting Vern's hand on his coffee mug, sad.

"I believe you too, Vern," I chimed in, figuring I might as well, just for the heck of it, even though I wasn't sure I believed Vern's ridiculous tree-in-the-prison-cell story.

"It's not that," said Vern. "No, nothing like that. I just feel funny that folks think I'm imaginative when all I did was tell it how it really was. I don't deserve any of these crazy accolades."

"You're a good man, Vern," said Helen and turned to me. "Has Vern gotten his ticket yet this evening?"

"Nope I haven't," Vern interjected.

"Your ticket is another simple one. Ready? Just repeat after me. *I am a good man!*"

The Sad Kitchen is a home for deliverance. Sadness is a steady disease, and it can be as cozy as the autumn, which is why it is so dangerous I think. Folks just get used to it.

It got to where we had passed out all 50 copies of Vern's book over the course of two weeks.

We didn't even have 50 customers before that point in time. Vern's children's book was becoming a great hit. Our regular customers were requesting multiple copies for other peoples' children, I suppose. Word must get around in children's circles: preschool and elementary school and all those other childhood enterprises. I don't know—children are beyond my area of expertise. Sometimes I forget they still exist.

This book which I'm making right now is getting further and further from childhood, I fear.

By the third week of Vern's book's publication, so to speak, we were still getting requests from our regular customers.

And not only were we getting lots of requests from our *regular* customers, we were getting more and more *new* customers. We were up to approximately twenty regulars, twenty-

29

five. And on any given night we might have had thirty-five customers throughout the whole of the night's shift. It was getting to where I couldn't keep folks straight, which, as a waiter, is my main task. I pride myself on knowing a name and a face and a tidbit about each of the customers of the Sad Kitchen.

A few of the new folks were:

-A gastroenterologist named Dominic Spencer (Sad news to come about him)

-A crew of lawncare professionals

-Three dental hygienists, all friends

-Herold, a high school basketball referee

-A self-proclaimed philosopher who claimed that the universe was shaped like a donut.

-A priest (one of Helen's old friends)

-A city council member

-Two fellows who called themselves "Lowriders" which is a term I am not familiar with in reference to human beings, only automobiles.

All this sudden growth prompted a lot more coffee, more cartons of eggs, and another batch of Vern's book that folks could bring home to their children.

This time, when my wife went into the print shop, instead of falling asleep in the car outside, I played a game with myself where I attempted to guess how big of a batch she would order. My guess was 75 copies, but I promised myself that if she went nuts and ordered 100 I absolutely would not say, "How much is all this costing us?"

My wife is a special person and she has her fingers on the tenderest spots of folks' souls: she ordered 250 copies of Vern's children's book about a tree growing up out of the floor of a little rabbit's timeout. Where would all these books go? We had nowhere close to that many customers. I guess Helen had a "Print it and they will come" approach to old Vern's book. The number dumbfounded me.

And Helen must have sensed this because she patted my thigh all the way home from the print shop that morning and that was all the communication we needed. Anything I attempted to say would have been inaccurate.

The reason Helen's (and Jack's) son was dead was that he was murdered during a robbery on the outskirts of his college campus. He was murdered by one of the guys in my ward.

She liked to visit the man—"Crank" as he was known around the ward, although his real name was Cliff—because she was trying to convince Cliff that she had forgiven him. It was a difficult thing to do and required much persistence, Helen told me after I was released from prison and we struck up a romance and eventually got married, aged 54 (me) and 49 (her).

Forgiving Cliff was an ongoing process until about a year ago. It was always a source of much frustration for Helen because no matter how much headway she made one week, she could come back the next week to find Cliff in a very dark place (a place of crippling guilt), all of her previous week's hard work unraveled.

The reason forgiving Cliff is no longer an ongoing process is that Cliff died about a year ago. The forgiving process is over and now it's just a matter of praying for him, so says Helen.

But I only learned about this terrible, horrible, intimate, magnificent connection between Cliff and Helen once I was already out of prison and long-gone into the throes of love with Helen and she opened up to me. Back when she used to visit Cliff and the rest of the guys on his ward, the topic Helen and I would discuss was her son and she would speak to me about him, very lovingly, as if he were still alive. The kid had been a shortstop in high school, and Helen would speak about him as if he were still playing shortstop in high school.

Shortstop is what we bonded over, Helen and me. I myself had been a shortstop. Thus, one embarrassing and very sad situation developed over the years: every week, when Helen would come visit the prison, I would give her a tip to relay to her son about how to make himself into a better shortstop. All that time, she never told me that her son was dead, and I just kept giving her those tips, week after week. "Tell that shortstop of yours to get his glove out in front of him when he goes to field a ground ball or else it'll eat him up." "Tell that shortstop of yours to kick some dirt around whenever there is a man on second base. Baserunners hate it! It gets in their head."

I can only assume it made her cry on her drives home from visiting the prison when she got in the car and realized she had no shortstop at home to relay those tips to. I didn't realize the situation, but that doesn't make me feel like any less of a tactless old fool.

An arrest occurred. It wasn't but two days after the printing of our 250-batch that a middle-aged fellow with a frog face came into the Sad Kitchen. We had only barely opened for the night. The coffee was still brewing, for heaven's sake.

"How does this place work?" he said to me, looking rather froggy.

"Well—" I said.

"I might need you to hurry," he said, in the slowest voice imaginable.

Then there was a silence. It was just him and me in the Sad Kitchen. No customers had arrived yet and my wife was in the back, cracking eggs. As I studied his face, I half-expected him to go *ribbit ribbit*. Instead, he used words: "Can you hide me?"

He looked almost bored.

"Hide you?" I was going to say, but I didn't get the chance, because next I knew two officers had burst through the door and slammed the frog-man's frog-face on our counter and were cuffing him and telling him his rights. I am ashamed to admit that the thing I was thinking when the cops put the man's face on our counter was: *Don't get frog guts on my clean counter!*

Two mornings later I saw the man's froggy mug in the newspaper. Unbelievable: he was some sort of bigwig doctor. He was a gastroenterologist named Dominic Spencer from the university hospital and he had been caught taking advantage of sedated patients behind closed doors in the worst way imaginable. The hospital had caught him on camera and he tried to flee.

Evidently this Dominic Spencer fellow had heard about the Sad Kitchen and mistook us as some sort of asylum for men fleeing the law. The newspaper didn't mention us in their article, but we wouldn't avoid the spotlight for long. Dominic Spencer was about to fall from grace, and he was going to try to use the Sad Kitchen as a wet mattress to soften his blow.

CHAPTER TWO

Vern had used crayons to paint the pictures for his children's book. Vern was NOT a good artist. He used stick figures for the creatures, and for everything that wasn't just a simple stick figure (such as the tree) he colored outside the lines—and there were no lines!

During the weeks when our batch of 250 books was being depleted, another new customer approached me very early one evening—around 8 p.m. This fellow was an artist, he said. Some of his work was in a gallery downtown, he said. The artist had a dark, soulful presence, and he used that presence to tell me, "I've got a proposition for you concerning the drawings in that book," while I filled his coffee cup.

He didn't come right out and state his proposition, but it was apparent where this was headed. "I'm not the decision maker of this operation," I said, topping him off. "One moment please."

I went and grabbed my wife.

They went to the end of the counter to talk. My wife's face had been a little bothered when I told her the situation, so I tried to remain nearby their conversation. If something unpleasant needed to occur, I would take it upon myself to become the unpleasantness. My willingness to be unpleasant on my wife's behalf is one of the most pleasant things about me, in my humble opinion.

"...I'm not going to touch any of the wording, just the art," was the statement coming out of the artist's mouth when I went to check on my wife.

My wife turned to me. Her mouth said, "This nice fellow is offering to revamp the pictures in Vern's book. And he also says he knows some people who would be willing to have it published afterward," but, while her mouth was saying these things, I was trying to listen to her eyes. Her eyes said, *I'm not so sure about this.*

"Vern's not in yet this evening," I offered up. "Should we wait and see what he thinks about all this?"

This statement was the perfect ground for my wife to stand on. "That's probably only fair to Vern," said my wife patting my chest. Then turning to the artist, "And I will say, I think there's something very honest about the way Vern did his pictures. I'm not sure they could be improved with all the talent in the world. Oh sure, you might make them very lovely, but we have the honest truth to consider. To redo those pictures might be like telling a fib in a prayer. Who are we fooling?"

"I understand completely," said the artist fellow. "Listen, you talk to Vern this evening and think things over, and I'll come back same time tomorrow, not because I want an answer but because I feel at home here." And for a moment, I believed him. For a moment, I thought he truly felt the spirit of my wife and of the Sad Kitchen and wasn't just looking for money or pride or whatever else.

When Vern arrived in the wee hours of that very night, my wife and I sat down with him at a booth and my wife sat on the same side of the booth as Vern so that it wouldn't feel like an inquisition or a parole hearing for poor Vern. In truth, Vern was carrying himself a little tentatively and with very hunched shoulders these days, ever since the second batch of his book came into being. His children's book had become something of a real-life child, and Vern was the stressed-out parent, hesitant to release his child to the world but aware that he needed to for the sake of the child AND for the sake of the world.

Folks made comments to Vern from one of two categories these days: category one, they praised and admired and congratulated his wild imagination, or, category two, they asked Vern, "Hey Vern, a tree didn't *really* grow up through the floor of your prison cell, did one?" Both of these categories of comments left Vern totally and completely trapped inside himself.

Ever gentle, with her hand on Vern's forearm, my wife explained the artist's offer. When she told Vern the bit about having the book certifiably published, Vern looked at me with terrified, trembling eyes.

"What do you think I should do, Miss Helen?"

"Well, Vern, this is your book—your creation!—and I don't think I should influence your decision one way or the other."

"Did he seem like an alright fellow?"

My wife thought for a moment. "The impression he gave seemed very earnest, yes, and I think it's only fair that we trust that impression."

But all three of us seated in that booth knew very well that my wife wouldn't speak badly about a fellow human being even if that fellow human being were holding a gun to her temple, threatening, "Hey lady, I want to hear you admit that I'm a piece of shit or else I'll pull the trigger and prove it to you." Vern looked at me for my read on the artist. "Bubba?" he said.

"Well Vern, at first I feared he was after money or whatever else, but like my wife said, he left a decent impression. You know how tough it can be to gauge a fellow's intentions."

Poor Vern was completely overwhelmed. "Let me get you some more coffee, Vern," I said, standing to grab the carafe. "A nice, sad cup, how about?"

We discussed the situation with Vern for almost an hour that night. There were, I believe, two points of serious intrigue for Vern.

Point of intrigue number one: if the artist repainted all of Vern's lousy but wholesome drawings, then some of the unwanted attention

Vern was dealing with might be redirected to the artist.

Point of intrigue number two: if the book were certifiably published, it could possibly make a little bit of money, some of which would fall into Vern's lap.

There was, however, one point of serious concern for poor Vern: "If that thing gets certifiably published," said Vern, "then my name and my story will really be out there."

"In a lot of ways it already is out there, Vern," I said in the interest of practicality.

"I mean out *there*," said Vern turning and jabbing a finger in the direction of the door of the Sad Kitchen, the alleyway outside, downtown, the world beyond.

The Sad Kitchen is a nurturing place. It's false that only the youth need nurturing. Most of the tickets are fairly simple: *Bring a plate of food to a homeless man and have a friendly talk with him. Say a rosary. Stare at a crucifix and think about your problems. Do some fasting. Go to mass at the St. Joseph Cathedral downtown* (even if you aren't Catholic). *Go chat with the priest during Confession* (even if you aren't Catholic). *Stick a special intention on our corkboard of intentions* (Jack let us store this in a closet) *and pray for all the intentions on the board. Give some alms if you can spare any.*

Sometimes Helen will personalize them the way she did for Vern when he wanted to do something for the children. Sometimes Mike's (with Tourettes) ticket would be to *Tell that girlfriend of yours that you love her*, or *Tell that girlfriend of yours that you're sorry.*

Vern entered the Sad Kitchen the next night in his finest attire. He had his hair slicked over and was wearing an old tie that must have been from the days of his trial. I guess he thought his decision regarding his book's destiny was important (which it was), and he wanted to dress for the occasion.

"Damn, Vern!" yelled Mike as soon as Vern entered, which incited quite a stir of hysteria among our patrons about Vern's appearance. But Vern was in no mood for enduring flattery.

He was very confident and serious when he asked me to get my wife. All I had to do was poke my head through the bat-wing doors and say, "Hey, Helen, I don't really know how to say this, so I'll just come right out and say it: Vern is here and he's wearing a tie." My wife came right away, looking quite concerned.

"Miss Helen," said Vern, with unshakable resolve, "I'm going to let that artist fellow revamp the pictures in my book and get that thing certifiably published," he told my wife.

"Vern, Sweetheart—"

"And one other thing, Miss Helen," said Vern. "If I happen to make a single penny off that thing..."

"Yes, Vern?"

"I'm going to have it donated to the children of this charity." Vern produced a greasy paper with the name of a charity on it from his jacket pocket and unfolded it and placed it on the counter and poked it with his finger.

In proud moments like this, my wife thinks about her son, the shortstop, and her son more than anything is the reason she cries. My wife was proud of Vern, and I suspect her shortstop son was more alive in her heart than he had been in a long time.

Over the course of the next few months, the artist worked on the re-creation of the pictures in Vern's book.

Many long nights they spent conversing over a cup of coffee in a corner booth, Vern and the artist. The artist wanted to thoroughly understand Vern's vision. Let me give the artist his due credit for that.

Of course, folks were very warm and embracing toward the artist. Such is the Sad Kitchen way!

My wife never gave the artist any tickets other than, *Keep working on those paintings!*

Mike—crazy, loudmouthed Mike—had a nickname for the artist: *Pa-sock-o.*

"Hey, Pa-sock-o! How are them paintings coming?" Mike would shout.

We were all confused by the nickname until we put it together: Mike meant "Picasso," but, Mike being the goofball that he is, got mixed up and called him "Pa-sock-o." It would have been embarrassing if it weren't so ridiculous.

In truth, these were a fine couple of months. It was autumn and we were cozy. The paintings were under development and Vern's spirits were high and his stress levels were low now that the artist had gained his trust and he felt his book was in good hands and folks' attention was shifted to the artist's progress.

Otherwise, there is very little to report from this period of time. We were getting a lot of new customers and the 250-batch of Vern's book was being further and further depleted. There were too many new faces for me to even pretend to recognize folks. I just had to be friendly about it.

Nowadays, my wife and I were going to mass more than ever. Typically, we went on Saturday nights on our way downtown to fulfill our Sunday obligation and it wasn't uncommon for us to catch one or two weekday masses per week on the drive home from the Sad Kitchen in the morningtime. But nowadays my wife was insisting on going three, even four times during the week in addition to our Sunday obligation.

During the weekday masses, after a long night's shift, I never failed to fall asleep in the pew. The priest was a young fellow who couldn't stop touching the bridge of his eyeglasses up on the altar. The only way for me to get him to stop touching the bridge of his glasses was to fall asleep.

My wife insisted on waiting around in the gathering space after mass to talk to the nervous kid. As they talked, I would just linger ten feet distant and fall asleep standing up. "Morning, Bubba," the young priest would always peek around my wife and wave to me.

"Morning, Father."

"Sorry for keeping you awake this morning," he'd say.

"Don't worry, you didn't."

Or, "Hey Bubba," the young priest would say, "what was my sermon about this morning?"

"About 10 minutes too long, Father," I'd say.

It was our little routine, and I suppose it was nice in its own small way. The sarcasm was a necessary part of any conversation in which I was expected to call a kid half my age "Father." Anyway, he was just a good kid who couldn't stop pushing on the bridge of his eyeglasses.

This period of time must have been quieter and slower than I initially realized since I find myself here discussing the nervous habits of a priest and his spectacles. But I suppose there is one very important thing to report: Dominic Spencer was quickly becoming the most hated man in the city. He even garnered some national hatred. His froggy mug tarnished the front page of The Dispatch, our city's newspaper, every single morning. It got to where The Dispatch, with a horrible ominous tone, referred to him only as "The Doctor." This nomenclature trickled down into folks' conversations at the Sad Kitchen. For better or for worse, we folks of the Sad Kitchen have a preoccupation with the news. In a few weeks, The Doctor's trial would begin.

On Thanksgiving night, we had a feast. It was the grand unveiling of the artist's rendering of the paintings for Vern's book. The paintings were hung in frames and placed in sequence around the Sad Kitchen like an art gallery.

"No tickets tonight!" my wife kept bursting through the bat-wing doors and announcing, waving kitchen implements like wands. "Just enjoy the feast and the wonderful display and be grateful!"

What a cheerful night—one of the Sad Kitchen's proudest moments. There was some thin sliced turkey and creamy gravy and mashed potatoes and pumpkin pie, all of this paid for by Jack, the owner of Jack's Diner. All the food was just a continuation of the Sad Kitchen itself, an attempt to grow softer and more tender to the human condition.

My wife always says that a sense of fullness can't be properly understood without hunger, and that it is impossible to be grateful until you are properly dependent, and that hatred is nothing but a secret hunger for love.

Folks were very impressed with the artist's pictures, especially since they had all read Vern's story and thus were familiar with the narrative.

Vern, for his part, maintained the look of a proud father not wanting to steal the spotlight from his child: his story. "You doing okay, Vern?" I found an opportunity to ask.

"Bubba," he said. "Do you know what the most challenging part of my life is these days?"

"What's that Vern?"

"Convincing myself that a human being like that wife of yours can exist without a catch. Is there a catch? Tell me there is a catch and I'll be able to sleep at night."

His statement caught me off guard the way most meaningful statements do. Because I knew exactly what he meant.

"Sometimes I look for it under her pillow," I joked. "I check her medicine cabinet. I watch her pray from the other room to see if a halo appears."

We had a good hearty laugh. "Or some wings," joked Vern.

Later, around two in the morning, the artist hopped on the counter and thanked everyone in the house. There were probably 50 or so people that night, I would estimate, although it is difficult to apply facts and figures to memories that feel barely real.

The artist up on the counter thanked Vern and raised a cup of coffee, sad, as a sort of toast for Vern's effort. The artist said what a profound pleasure it had been to get to know Vern and said that he never really understood what it meant to create a painting until he set out to create the paintings for Vern's children's book. "There is something about simplicity that is very, very complicated unless your heart is in the right place," said the artist. Then, turning directly to Vern as the house grew silent and contemplative: "Vern, you are a good man."

Soon afterward, the artist left the Sad Kitchen, presumably to go get the book published. But we wouldn't hear from him for months.

CHAPTER THREE

This was the start of a long winter. The Christmas season can be difficult for folks of the Sad Kitchen. Helen always tries to romanticize the modesty of the nativity scene in the quiet nights of the Sad Kitchen. "Our job in this life is to try our best to create the nativity scene the way Mary and Joseph did: bring Jesus into the world in our own modest way in the quietest corners of the world!" But folks inevitably get their hopes up with visions of extravagance and grandeur.

Vern felt left in the dark concerning the destiny of his book—vulnerable and exposed. It was as if his child were in surgery while he was forced to sit in the waiting room: a stool at the counter of the Sad Kitchen. He waited and wondered and worried.

For months, his tickets had involved his book—making it and reading it and helping the artist grasp his vision—but now Vern was receiving tickets of old. *Go give a plate of food to a lonely friend on a bench. Pray a rosary. Call your daughter even though she says she hates you and is ashamed.* These tickets, I believe, felt like a terrible backslide for Vern. He used to be proud of those sorts of tickets but now I think he associated them with failure and with the fact that his book was "out *there.*"

Another arrest occurred. This was out in the alleyway just outside the doorway of the Sad Kitchen and just beyond the reach of the moonlight. The glinting light of the police car slammed and wailed soundlessly against the glass pane of the front door of the Sad Kitchen and inside all was silent. All had been silent beforehand, but now there was a new, more purposeful silence. Folks sat hunched over their plates and their coffee mugs out of reverence.

I can recall similar such reverent silences from nights in prison.

When my wife detected the shift in the silence, she came through the bat-wing doors and said, "What's wrong?" And then she saw the blue-red glinting on the front door and joined the silence and stood and prayed.

The person being arrested was another one of our newer customers, a fellow who had joined us not long after the second batch of Vern's book was printed. Kurt was his name. Sometimes his "Old Lady" (as he called her) came along, a pregnant woman named Janice. I wouldn't normally use that terminology, "Old Lady," because Helen has banned its usage. For example, Mike used to call his girlfriend "the Old Lady" but Helen disallowed it. "Are you married to this woman, Michael?" Helen asked him when he spoke of his Old Lady.

"No, Ma'am."

"Well in here, she will be known as your girlfriend or your better half."

"Yes, Ma'am."

But Kurt and Janice were new, and Helen

hadn't overheard Kurt use the term yet and I didn't have the spine Helen had for correcting folks.

When Kurt first used the term "Old Lady," to introduce his wife, I said, "Are you all married?"

Kurt said, "I just told you. She's my *Old Lady*," and then gave a big wink. It was a little humorous or at least ironic because Janice was a small and young-looking woman, and nothing about her screamed *Old Lady*.

"I'll give you fair warning," I said, "Miss Helen doesn't exactly approve of that terminology. *Old Lady*."

"Who is Miss Helen?" said Kurt.

"She's the angel of this operation. My wife."

"Well maybe I'll start calling my Old Lady here *'Miss Janice'*. How's that?"

"Or Angel Janice!" said Janice looking shy and rubbing her womb—very precious.

But Kurt went right back to calling Janice his Old Lady and I never corrected him again because I've become soft in my old age and, besides, I very much liked Kurt and Janice right from the start. Individually they were special, but together they brought with them a third, even more special presence (Janice's womb was part of this third presence, but not the whole of it).

Janice wasn't there the night that Kurt got arrested which, at the time, the rest of us considered a silver lining. It wasn't until later—weeks or months—that we found out the sad truth of the matter: Janice had been arrested at their apartment earlier in the night and now it was Kurt's turn. Evidently, they were wanted by the law for a great deal of thievery that had taken place a few months prior in a city across the country. Now Kurt would go to a prison for men, Janice would go to a different prison for women, and I don't know where that third presence I spoke of earlier would go. I fear the answer is very far from childhood.

And the artist didn't come and didn't come. For Vern, every time the door opened, it was the artist not coming through the door.

Vern was withdrawn into the place of his life that had once been occupied by his children's book. It was a whining and weeping emptiness and he was perpetually trying to fill it with himself. He no longer greeted folks when they entered because, when they entered, they were not-the-artist. Vern wouldn't even meet folks' eyes. He looked at folks as if they were looking at him as a failure. Through folks' eyes—especially Helen's, I suppose—Vern saw himself as a failure. He went through the trouble of inhabiting other folks' eyes for the sole purpose of seeing himself as a failure who had once written a children's book but now was getting meek tickets of old.

The artist didn't come and didn't come, even after the Christmas season was through.

Helen was troubled because she didn't know what to do about Vern. Mopey, mopey Vern. Meanwhile, Vern had stopped coming to the Sad Kitchen every night—he would come only three, maybe four nights per week these days.

It just so happened he was there the night the artist finally did return with a publishing contract for Vern to sign. But by the time the artist came back (publishing contract in hand), everything was all different. It was like the story of the prodigal son had been made victim of its own beauty right under the nose of my dear poor wife, for the artist expected to burst through the doors and have it be like Thanksgiving Part Two—a party. And I think the rest of us folks would have liked for it to be that way too, but we had to defer to Vern and, for Vern, everything was all different. The joy of his children's book was gone. His face was like the porcelain of an empty mug and there was nothing for me to do except pour it full of the saddest coffee.

Outside it was a new year and there was no way of faking our situation in the Sad Kitchen. Vern and the artist went to a corner booth and signed the papers, and then the two of them—Vern and the artist—got into a spat. As these things happen, it began as a verbal altercation:

"There, go make yourself famous," said Vern tossing his pen at the artist's face.

"Right, because mixing my reputation with a criminal is a quick route to glory," said the artist.

"You need this place worse than any of us," said Vern.

"What the hell's that supposed to mean?" said the artist.

"You think you're above this place," said

Vern. "You think you're our savior. But we don't need you. We've got Miss Helen."

"Miss Helen is the one who told us to work together in the first place you ungrateful piece of dog shit," said the artist. "Every night my ticket was to sit in this booth and work with you. Do you think Miss Helen would have given me that ticket if she didn't know what a supreme pain in the ass you are to work with?"

"Miss Helen was just doing you a favor, Jackass," said Vern. "She knew you wouldn't humble yourself so she was trying to do the work for you by letting you work with me, because I'm the salt of the earth. But you still ignored her grace and left us, you proud little prick."

"If you're the salt of the earth then no wonder this life is so damned flavorless," muttered the artist under his breath, and then chuckled.

These sorts of disputes follow a strict format with which I am all too familiar; I had been waiting for a certain cue. In this case, the cue was the artist's under-his-breath comment followed by a chuckle. The chuckle had given this spat the ignition it needed to express itself physically at any moment. I leapt over the counter and tried to hold back old angry mopey vulnerable Vern.

My attempt at peacekeeping worked, but for all the wrong reasons. It only worked because I tripped and fell and wrenched my back. Down for the count I was. And I was quivering—how useless and embarrassing.

Folks all took a knee around me while Helen came up and whispered in my ear and then shouted, "Someone call an ambulance!"

Something was knocked loose in my spine and I couldn't stop trembling and convulsing. Never before had I so completely lacked possession of this thing which I have come to call myself. It felt like my brain was trying to instruct an imaginary limb to knit my spine back together. I could detect, unmistakably, a difference between my mind and my body and myself. "Are you in there, Bubba?" Helen whispered to me, and the question was too complicated to answer just then.

The ambulance came, but a cop did as well.

It was the middle of the night and here we were in a back alley and a man (me) was lying like the most pathetic docked fish on the floor of a questionable (albeit friendly) operation, and it would be an understatement to say that the cop was suspicious.

"What's going on here?" I heard the cop say while I was being loaded onto a stretcher.

Helen was ushering folks out. She had decided to close the Sad Kitchen early so that she could accompany her pathetic groom to the hospital.

"What exactly is this place?" I heard the officer say.

"Everybody, everybody," Helen announced. "I'm sorry but we are going to have to shut down for the night."

Meanwhile, two men were loading me into an ambulance in the cold night and I was trying to figure out whether the coldness I was feeling was of mind, body, or spirit. A paramedic's crotch was right in my face and I couldn't do anything about it because my neck was malfunctional. Everything was all mixed up because of the wrench in my spine.

The evacuation process incited a lot of stress and chaos, and, as these things go, it launched

Mike with Tourettes into quite an episode. "I punched her gut!" he was screaming. "I took my knee and put it in her face!" His screams filled the alleyway and garnered the attention of the policeman.

But the last thing I remember before the ambulance doors closed, even in the midst of Mike's terrible filibuster, was Valli crying to Helen, and then screaming *at* Helen. Valli didn't want to spend a night on the cold hard streets of downtown, and she was taking her frustration out on my wife.

Then the ambulance doors closed and everybody was gone.

I felt like a fool, and old. I had been injured in fights before, but always in dignified ways— having a tooth knocked out or an eye socket ruptured, things that didn't force me to wonder about the difference between my mind, body, and soul.

I woke up in the hospital the next morning thinking about Mike. "What happened with Mike?" I said, still coming awake.

I turned to Helen. The white light of a bright morning in a hospital room after my long sleep was very conducive to Helen's appearance as an angel, which she was. She had a sad face. "How do you feel, Bubba?"

"I think I can feel my body again," I said. I hadn't tried moving yet, but now I did, and it felt as if icicles were shattering inside my ribs. "As much as I would rather not," I added, out of breath from the pain.

Helen took my hand.

"What happened with Mike?" I said.

"Well I don't know how much you saw, but that officer wanted to arrest him."

"Arrest him on what grounds!" I said, trying to be angry, but it hurt too much.

She squeezed my hand with both of hers and bowed her head and closed her eyes and vanished into prayer. I tried to go with her, but my eyes wouldn't fall shut.

The last time I woke up in a hospital, I was handcuffed to the bed. I was twenty-seven years old, and it was the morning after my arrest. I'd been the getaway driver for a group of buddies in their attempt to burglarize a gas station. We were a clever bunch.

The reason I woke up in the hospital instead

of in jail was that, about 30 feet into our getaway, I accidentally veered the vehicle into a gas pump at a very swift rate of speed.

I was the only one severely injured, although it could be said that both the getaway vehicle and the gas pump were casualties.

The reason my eyes wouldn't fall shut now, even in the presence of Helen's nurturing grace, was that I was calling to mind the pictures of the demolished gas pump from my court case all those years ago. The gas pump was totally wrecked. It looked like a creature suspended in the worst agony, I seem to recall.

But it was just a gas pump, right? Well, I don't know. I've thought about it a lot and I have concluded that, in the grand scheme of my life, that gas pump might represent something far more complicated than your face-value gas pump. If I ever start to feel myself riding a moral high horse behind the counter at the Sad Kitchen, I remind myself that that gas pump could just as easily have been a man—a father of two young children or some such tragic situation. It was only dumb luck that that gas pump wasn't a man, because there is something else I have neglected to mention about my role as a getaway driver in a gas station burglary: I was drunk.

Finally, my eyes were closed. Helen's hands were warm on mine.

The machines that the folks at the hospital hooked me up to and inserted me into all beeped very stupidly, and it came as no surprise that they couldn't figure out the meaning of the pain I was experiencing. It was a strange, contradictory situation: the more pain I was in, the uglier and stupider the machines became which they stuck me inside of, and the more adamantly they claimed I was in perfect health. All day long, doctors and nurses were making inconclusive comments about things which I didn't understand the meaning of, until eventually they told me I was being discharged, which was something that I was able to understand.

"Take ibuprofen as needed. Otherwise, just stay off your feet, but don't lie down for too long either."

"What am I supposed to do, hover?"

The doctor thought I was making a joke, the pompous jerk.

The pain was tricky because it seemed to have no focal point. I lay on the couch at our apartment trying to make sense of it. If you told me to point to it, I wouldn't be able to. I would begin by indicating the region of my rib cage, but no, that wasn't quite true. Sometimes it slipped up to my neck and sometimes it traveled, vaguely, down my leg. Sometimes it seemed to originate in my back, sometimes in my chest. Sometimes it seemed to originate from a place that was altogether outside of my body.

The pain itself seemed to be having an identity crisis, not just with its origin, but with the way in which it expressed itself. More than pain, it felt like a clash of forces: heat versus cold, pressure versus numbness.

It was a week before I was back at my duties at the Sad Kitchen, and two weeks before I was worth a darn. But even then I couldn't stand for more than ten minutes before my leg turned hot and numb, as if invisible wax were melting and then pouring down my leg. I kept having to sit down and catch my breath.

Meanwhile, the trial of Dominic Spencer, the gastroenterologist, "The Doctor," was in full swing. The Dispatch loved to print pictures of him in his orange jumper with his hands chained and his froggy mug looking bored and hate-worthy, and I loved to look at those pictures because they were an easy object on which to project the wickedness of my pain.

But on the third or fourth day of the trial, Dominic Spencer's lawyer, in an attempt to convince the media that his boy was a good man who merely suffered from an addiction, made a certain comment to a reporter from The Dispatch after the trial recessed for the day: "Consider this: Where was the first place he went when he felt the guilt of his actions? Darn it if he didn't go to a soup kitchen! He went to a soup kitchen downtown to devote time to his community! A place of community service! Are these the actions of a monster? No! I urge you to see the full-picture here, ladies and gentlemen."

The Dispatch article went on to mention that the soup kitchen was only an unverified, underground establishment known as...(here it came, folks, our name would be officially out *there*, to use Vern's terminology)…the Sad Kitchen.

All of a sudden the name of the Sad Kitchen and the lies of Dominic Spencer were appearing in the same news article.

Now comes the period of time when the police made it a habit to drive slowly past the Sad Kitchen and through the alleyway several times per night. At least once per night an officer entered the Sad Kitchen to heft his trousers and touch his belt buckle. If you offered him a seat and some coffee, he'd turn up his bottom lip and turn around and leave. But his point was made: over the last few months we had had two arrests, one of which was the wretched and hated Dominic Spencer, and a third incident involving my wrenched back, and now we were officially on the police's radar.

Plus, there was Vern's trouble weighing us down. After he signed that contract, it was as if Vern were perpetually leaving the Sad Kitchen. It seemed every time I looked at the door, there was poor mopey Vern, leaving without ever having talked to anyone. Who knew a man could depart from an establishment more often than he could arrive in the first place?

Helen didn't know what to do about it, and I knew she didn't know what to do about it, and yet we never discussed it. There were important things that needed to be discussed and, as a replacement for those important things, I would make the most obvious and meaningless statement in the world, "We're getting too old for this, Helen." And in reply my wife would ask the most obvious, meaningless question, "How is your back, Bubba?"

In this small way we avoided everything we needed to discuss: Vern's sadness, the recent arrests, the suspicious police, the fact that our customer base had increased and we were therefore creating quite a financial imposition on poor Jack, and of course the fact that we were getting old and my spine was wrenched.

My wife's prayer was more fervent than ever these days. Her face disappeared into her prayer. We came home from the Sad Kitchen and right away I lay down on the couch to rest my sorry spine while Helen went straight into our bedroom and prayed, kneeling there against the bed.

I set out writing this account with the intention to be nothing but honest, so I'll mention for honesty's sake that my wife's fervent prayer had begun to infuriate me a little bit during this dark period of time. The sound of her tiny prayerful whispers had begun to tiptoe and then to ballet and then to tap-dance about the edges of my pain.

"Helen," I'd call in there to end the whispers.

"Yeah, Bubba?"

"We're getting too old for this." What else was there to say?

"How's your back, Bubba? Can I get you anything?"

It went on and on like that in the wintertime so that my wife's face was no longer a face, but just an image of herself kneeling in prayer as viewed from my reclined vantage on the couch. "I feel extra old today, Helen."

"Why don't I get you some ibuprofen for that back of yours?"

Until one day I had run out of ways to express how old we were becoming and how deeply

I was in pain, and something terrible erupted from my stupid mouth. She was in there praying very fervently and I was feeling extra agitated. "You're wasting your damn time!" I belted, as if my back pain were manifesting itself as the words of a daemon.

"Bubba?" said Helen.

"You heard me. Either your prayers aren't working or you're asking for all the wrong shit!"

She came over to me with her face missing— just a cloudy image of her kneeling in prayer in its place. Then she sat down and rested my head on her lap and said, "Would you like to pray with me, Bubba?" and I felt how lovely her voice really was. What an ointment! What a salve! It was the most soothing balm. I felt like a child.

"I don't think so," I said, which turned me back into a curmudgeon.

"Please," she urged, cupping my hand and leading me once more into my childhood.

"Do you ever consider the possibility," I asked, trying to maintain a steady voice, "that this prayer business amounts to nothing but a superstitious racket? Don't you ever worry that you are just babbling to the atmosphere? I mean to say, don't you ever consider the possibility that your whole operation is finally, utterly bull shit?"

"Dear God," she said, very calmly closing her eyes in prayer, "sometimes we feel like aimless, wandering madmen speaking to the air. Please give us faith. Amen."

"Well that's nice and patronizing, isn't it?" I said, sitting up and looking her dead in the face, which was so peaceful that I had the urge to throw a rock at it. "I mean seriously, Helen, do you understand Vern's crime? Have you ever used the rational corner of your brain to really think about it all the way down through to the depths of its horribleness? If you are ignoring the gravity of this situation, it's not just *oopsie*! It's not just *oh, fiddlesticks*! You are an evil, evil witch of a woman."

"Dear God," she said, looking down at her hands which were balled up ostentatiously in her little lap, "sometimes we worry that you sent your Son only part of the way into our mess rather than all the way down into the very depths of it. Please give us hope. Amen."

"I would like to admit," I said, speaking very slowly now, and tasting deliciously every word, "that I do not understand what you stand for. I do not know what I am standing for when I stand next to you as your husband."

"Dear God," she said, and her face was gone, vanished, "give us love."

"Woman!" I shouted. "I'm trying to talk to you!"

"God!" she shouted even louder. "I'm trying to talk to you!"

"WHERE IS GOD!" I blasted gloriously. "WHERE IS GOD IN A SITUATION LIKE THIS? LISTEN! DO YOU HEAR THAT? NOTHING! NOWHERE!"

CHAPTER FOUR

It was only a few days later that we arrived at the Sad Kitchen for an evening shift to find a hardbound copy of Vern's book waiting for us near the stove alongside a note that said, "Channel 4 tomorrow night at eleven." The note was signed by the artist.

Helen picked up the book. *Timeout for Vernon.* She opened the cover and it made a smooth greasy sound like the click of water lapping gently on a seashore. Clearly this book had never been opened before and it reeked a fresh and self-conscious little odor. I stood over Helen's shoulder and cupped my hands on her elbows as she held the book. She was a little bit mesmerized. The first page inside the front cover was all white except for a short passage: a

72

dedication. "For Helen and all my friends at the Sad Kitchen who showed me where to find the Holy Spirit."

I wasn't sure if the dedication was Vern's touch or the artist's, but it must have been Vern's. The artist must have discussed the dedication with Vern during one of their long meetings in the corner booth about Vern's vision for his children's book and now here it was: a real artifact of love.

Together we read the book and there was nothing to say. Helen's hands were trembling the whole time she held the special thing, and that was all we needed in terms of communication. The artist had done a lovely job on the paintings, and I won't even attempt to explain what I mean by "lovely." What I mean by lovely can't be explained here in a book that is so distant from childhood. The more I would attempt to explain it here, the further my explanation would deviate from the childlike simplicity of the truth.

After we finished reading the book, talking once again seemed like a useful, rational activity. Jackhammering the snowfall of our silence, I said, "What do you suppose is going to be on Channel 4 tomorrow night?"

"I don't know, Bubba, but we had better figure out how to program that darn television."

A television hung behind the counter at the Sad Kitchen, but we had never turned it on. It was blaring constantly during Jack's Diner's hours of operation, but we always shut it off at the beginning of our Sad Kitchen shift because it was contrary to our purposes at the Sad Kitchen. But now we had an obvious need for it.

That night we forewarned all our Sad Kitchen customers that Vern's book had been certifiably published and bound with the artist's pictures and that something mysterious involving the book was going to be on the news tomorrow night and we were going to have a viewing party of sorts, so they should try to be here by 11 p.m. Folks were sure intrigued: Was Vern going to be on tv? Would he be at the viewing party tomorrow night? Better yet, both?

We just hoped it wasn't neither.

We didn't see Vern that night, and thus we—Helen and me—were left in the dark. But our lack of answers only provoked the mystery concerning tomorrow night's broadcast, because...

...Wow! Did folks sure show up. By 10 p.m. we had only been open for three hours and the house was packed: forty people, fifty. One man, a newer customer named Dwayne, brought six Tupperware containers full of cookies—144 cookies in total—which his wife had baked. Karen (the lawyer from the skyscraper) brought three enormous tubs of kettle corn, which I assume were left over from Christmas. Another man, a fellow I altogether did not recognize, attempted to have 10 cases of beer delivered in a van around 9 p.m., but before they could move the beer inside the establishment, Helen was outside in the alleyway putting her foot down. The Sad Kitchen needed to behave itself following the recent arrests and my wrenched back incident, and I guess Helen didn't think 240 cans of beer would be helpful to the situation.

Cookies and kettle corn were where Helen drew her line for the viewing-party-festivities.

By 10:30, the Sad Kitchen was humming with plenty of sugar, coffee, and neon light. Folks had been pleading for us to turn the lights down to foster a movie-theatre-type atmosphere, and when Helen obliged, and the lights went down, a neon beer sign from behind the counter that we had never paid much heed was all of a sudden the main attraction. The Sad Kitchen was aglow with a lunar blue warmth and an almost guttural whooping sound from the very excited audience. One question remained, and if you listened close enough to the general din of excitement, you would figure it out pretty quickly. It went like this: "Psst...pssssst... Vern...Where's old Vern?... pst... psssssssst... tsst....seen Vern?"

Indeed, old Vern had yet to arrive.

Concerning Vern, my concerns were twofold: One, I feared Vern *would* arrive and the house would erupt with such excitement as to cause structural damage to the Sad Kitchen or, two, I feared Vern would *not* arrive and we would have

76

to celebrate without him. I don't know which concern was more concerning at the time.

Regardless, around 10:45, almost as if he had a flair for the dramatic (which he didn't), Vern entered the Sad Kitchen. In hindsight, I suppose this was the last time he would step foot on our friendly premises.

If his mood upon entry was mopey or somber or if he was spooked by the size of the crowd, he didn't get a chance to express it, for, as I feared and expected, he was so suddenly assailed with adoration. Within seconds, cookies were being flung across the dining room and an entire tub of kettle corn was dumped over Vern's head and then folks began to bang on the aluminum jug, which was over Vern's head like a lampshade. It was a celebratory mobbing like after a walk-off home run in extra innings, but, little did folks realize, we were only in the sixth inning of this particular situation. All I could do was cringe, both because of the mess that was being made with the kettle corn and because I knew how sensitive Vern was about receiving attention, especially accolades.

But these folks needed and deserved something to celebrate. I think Helen realized that and therefore allowed it to continue.

I wanted to find Vern to talk to him, to gauge his emotional condition, but it was a difficult crowd to navigate and folks were requesting a great deal of coffee in our darkened establishment, and suddenly it was eleven p.m., and, under the blue light, a very electric silence had enforced itself—it gave me the impression that if I made any disruptive movements, a strong voltage would surge through us all. Vern was given a seat front and center at the counter before the television.

This next part is difficult. This next part is where the story entirely unhinges itself from the child that it once was and begins to think and act by itself and for itself. I can do nothing but tell it the way it happened.

The eleven o'clock news featured an interview with two news anchors—a lady in a dress that showed a lot of leg and a gentleman with shiny hair—and the artist (looking pretty ritzy, himself), all three of whom were seated on a

78

red couch. On a little coffee table before them was propped a copy of Vern's book alongside three coffee mugs. Sure, it was a nice setting, but in the family room of my soul, it struck me as a little ridiculous.

After a few news tidbits and the lottery drawing and a weather update and a few commercials, the lady with a lot of leg said: "With us this evening we have a local artist who has gone behind the scenes to work on a children's book with an ex-con. Now he comes forward to tell his story. Thank you for joining us, and blah blah blah blah blah…"

A wave of whooping and yucking passed through the Sad Kitchen.

On the tv, the interview began in a pleasant manner and the artist had a charming rapport with the anchors on the couch and folks were proud. But it was easy to discern a cynical purpose for this interview: the artist wanted to promote his new project and show folks what a sympathetic and open-minded fellow he was for dealing with such an untouchable guy as Vern.

But who can fault the artist for that? Because in truth he spoke very highly of Vern and of his experiences at the Sad Kitchen, how wholesome and loving and embracing and not-judgmental it is, and how it is a good way for troubled and guilt-ridden (except he kept throwing around the term "guilt neurosis" in order to sound snazzy, I guess) individuals to reestablish a connection with society. It was especially nice for him to attest to our reputation in the aftermath of its having been splattered with mud in association with the wretched frog Dominic Spencer.

And when the news team asked him about old Vern, the artist couldn't have had kinder words to describe his artistic partner. "Sometimes simplicity is exceedingly more complex than the most complicated complexity," the artist said about Vern, essentially juicing up his Thanksgiving toast. Meanwhile, here in the Sad Kitchen on the other side of the television, folks were coming up and squeezing Vern's shoulders or touching his arm or patting his back. They were respectful and didn't say anything. They knew it had been a trying time for him.

A cynical person would call the beginning part of the interview "simpering" or "self-serving," but being cynical is a lazy-hearted decision and I hereby declare the artist and the news anchors to be good folks who were only doing their jobs. On both sides of the screen, folks really were touched.

But then the gentleman anchor asked, very casually, "In the scope of your project, why don't you tell us a little bit about your co-author's conviction, and maybe, if you would, can you also offer a statement or a sentiment for any of our viewers whose lives have been touched by this type of child abuse?"

The artist was caught off guard. "What?" he said. "Pardon?"

The female anchor, looking back and forth between the artist and the camera, said, "We understand that your co-author's conviction involved several counts of sexual abuse of a minor, and—not to make this about his crime, because that's *not* what this is about—we were hoping you might offer a comment to victims of child abuse in light of this promising and truly hopeful work you've done with Mr. Richardson."

"I…" said the artist, a stuttering mess.

"Were you—" said the male anchor.

"No," said the artist. "I mean yes. I was unaware of the exact nature of Vern's crime." His words sounded like they belonged in a court room, not on a bright red couch with a coffee table. Apparently in all the artist's and Vern's discussions about Vern's vision for the

81

book, the reason for Vern's imprisonment all those years ago never came to light.

The news anchors looked at each other. The silence on the television became the silence in the Sad Kitchen.

The artist said nothing, so the female anchor took it upon herself to attempt to save all three of their dignities with a very false chuckle and some very pointless words: "It certainly wasn't our intention to catch you off guard—"

"It never came up," the artist cut her off. "I can honestly say it never came up between Vern and me. His crime or his sentence. Maybe it didn't interest me, I don't know. I would like to say it doesn't matter, I would like to say this changes nothing, but I think you can tell from my voice that that's not the case. I think you can hear in my voice that it changes everything."

The lady news anchor was nodding her head very seriously and then when she realized another silence had befallen the scene and that she was expected to fill it, she looked genuinely fearful, terrified for a moment. "We will move on then…" she started to say.

"I don't have a statement prepared at this time," the artist cut her off again with disgust in his voice. "This isn't something I'm prepared to speak about just now."

"Then how about we change directions for the time being and ask you to speak a little about your influences?" said the female anchor. "What were some of your favorite children's books growing up?"

The interview went on, but I'm sure it was only an attempt to save face.

As I turned from the television to check on Vern, the realization that he would already be gone took the wind right out of me. Indeed, Vern had left the Sad Kitchen. And the terrible suction of his departure was the aggregate of all the times he ever departed the Sad Kitchen. I should have gone after him that night, but I didn't. There was no wind in me, and there was no atmosphere for me to move through. Oh sure, a few folks went after him, but it didn't matter. He wasn't coming back.

I should have gone after him anyway, just for the sake of going after him, just for the sake of failing to bring him home.

The next morning we cleaned up the Sad Kitchen and didn't talk. Soon Jack's Diner would be open but there were thousands of soggy puffs of kettle corn adhered to the ground and we needed to clean them up.

It was Jack, Helen, a few other folks, and I who hung around to clean the kettle corn. Karen hung around, I guess since it was her kettle corn.

My back hurt.

I kept having to stand up and wipe drips of tears from my nose. When I stood up, I could hear the hum of the neon sign behind the counter. It was a deep hum and it felt like Satan himself was humming in my ear and massaging my shoulders every time I stood up to ease the pain. So I bent back over and the hum vanished but the pain started back up and once again the tears started to drip from my nose.

Meanwhile somewhere in a skyscraper, an article was being drafted. We could see the top third of The Dispatch building from the alleyway just outside the Sad Kitchen. At that moment, as we were chiseling smushed kettle corn, a reporter from The Dispatch was drafting an article to be dispatched about Vernon Richardson, and about the fact that he had only spent one year in prison for raping a minor. It was going to be referred to as a developing story.

They were going to start looking into his early parole, and into the leniency of our justice system in general. That was all being written somewhere up in the sky while we were scraping kettle corn off the absolute floor of the earth: the floor of the Sad Kitchen. The article would be published in two days' time.

What was Helen's condition that morning? I can't remember what we spoke about on the drive home after scraping the kettle corn. I can't begin to imagine or to conjure anything useful from the dregs of my memory.

As usual, the more complicated the situation became, the more at-peace Helen seemed to grow, and the simpler our conversations became, so probably our discussion that morning was something very small.

"Should we stop somewhere and get you a hot breakfast, Bubba?" she probably said.

"How about some kettle corn?" I probably joked.

She probably laughed sweetly.

As our situation became trickier and trickier, I was beginning to understand the value of a children's book. But no matter how hard I try, this book will never be a children's book. We went home and I slept all day while Helen prayed. Here I am trying to tell this story from my sleep and Helen is busy in prayer.

The very next night was when the police started monitoring the Sad Kitchen around the clock, open-to-close, with an on-duty officer in-house at all times. Needless to say, folks were very nervous and skittish and, pouring coffee into folk's mugs, I started to feel the need to talk with my eyes instead of my mouth, which is contradictory to everything the Sad Kitchen stood for. Talking with my eyes was something I learned in prison when times were tense.

Something awful occurred: As he typically does when there is tension in the air, Mike went on one of his Tourettes outbursts: "I punched her in the gut," and so on and so forth. Immediately the in-house police officer sat up so fast that his upward momentum sent his stool skidding into the wall behind him as he put Mike's face flat on the countertop and handcuffed him. Mike was shoved out of the Sad Kitchen, still having a fit. But his fit was a Tourettes-type fit where all he could say in protest was: "I put my knee to her gut! All of this in front of my little girl!"

In my memory now, as Mike is being dragged out of the Sad Kitchen, the door opens and I can hear cheering from the outside. Was this cheering real or is it the result of what, now, in hindsight, I know is coming?

Slap! said the newspaper when Jack dropped it on the counter before me at the beginning of the day's seventh hour. The Dispatch article had broken: "Awkward moment prompts 'good, hard look in the mirror of our justice system.'" The couch interview from Channel 4 was, of course, the "Awkward moment." The headline classified itself as a developing "story," the gist of which was trying to shed some light on the balance between early parole and justice. It involved a lot of statistics on various things: the overcrowding of prisons, the percentage of sentences that are served in-full, the number of repeat offenders relative to the length of sentence relative to percentage of sentence served relative to the nature of the crime (violent or non-violent) relative to gender of the offender relative to race of the offender relative to race of the victim relative to eye color relative to favorite type of music relative to whether the offender likes spicy food relative to whether he prefers boxers or briefs relative to blah blah blah blah blah. Pardon that little bit of sarcasm. My point is, Vern's situation was used strictly as a case study, a can-opener for a can of worms, where worms = statistical facts, figuratively speaking.

And speaking of "figuratively speaking," when the headline said it was taking a "look in the mirror," it actually meant it was going to "peer down its nose through the window of a skyscraper, judgmentally," because the real kicker is that the article used all of those wormy statistics to arrive at a very simple conclusion: Justice for violent criminals was not being served in our state prisons and our parole criteria were flawed.

In the blurb, the Sad Kitchen was referred to, but only in name, not location, and it was called an underground "Soup Kitchen," located in Jack's Diner, which was obviously a little misleading. But I suppose we should have enjoyed the false identity while we had the chance, because it was about to get even falser.

On the drive home that morning, instead of saying things like, "Does Jack think it's about time to shut down the Sad Kitchen?" or "Is Jack's business going to suffer because of all this?" I said things like, "I think I made the coffee a little weak last night."

"Oh yeah?" said Helen.

"I could see the bottom of the cup when I poured it."

"How's your back, Bubba?"

"I think it's a little better. Just keep praying, lady."

At home that morning I couldn't sleep so I went out to the parking lot to change the oil in our automobile while my wife was inside in prayer. A sedan with a *The Dispatch* emblem drove up and a young woman in a tan coat and heels got out of the sedan and looked at our little complex.

"Hello sir, do you know a woman by the

name of Helen Sampson?"

"Who is asking?" I said, being sure to keep my focus on the dipstick I was holding so The Dispatch lady would know that she did not merit my full attention.

She introduced herself as Melinda from The Dispatch while I pretended to study the dipstick even closer.

After she was done, I stood from under the hood of our automobile and let it slam shut like rifle fire. *BANG!* The Melinda lady jumped. I said, "Nope. No Helen Sampsons here."

"I'll just go knock on the door," she said, quickly gathering her dignity.

"Helen is my wife. She's not home."

"Bubba," said Helen. She had come out on our front balcony in plain sight.

"Yeah."

"What's going on down there? I heard a bang."

"This lady was looking for you. I was just explaining to her that you aren't home."

"Do you think she bought it?"

"Did you buy it?" I asked Melinda.

She smirked, very prim. Right away I could tell this was a woman I would have referred to as a "tough cookie" in the days before I met Helen and she told me to stop using that terminology.

"I don't think she bought it," I said.

"What was that awful bang I heard?" said Helen.

"She tried to shoot me," I said.

"Well come on inside, Sweetheart, and we can work on your aim," said Helen heading inside.

In our little kitchen it was my job to prepare the coffee while Melinda and Helen sat at our kitchen table and started talking. Before the coffee was even brewed, they had a secret rapport that I couldn't keep up with. Their discussion seemed to be taking place on two different plains or levels, only one of which I could understand. The other one was extremely complex and took place well-above my head.

"Thank you for welcoming me into your home, Mrs. Sampson," said Melinda.

"You're welcome, Melinda. You can call me Helen."

"I'm hoping to interview you for an editorial I plan to write about the Sad Kitchen."

"Well that's fine. I will answer as clearly as I can."

Meanwhile, I set down their coffee and stood prepared to defend my wife's honor, but I'm afraid I wound up watching them talk as if I were watching a tennis match, or ping pong.

"What is the Sad Kitchen?" said Melinda.

"It is a place for folks who can't live with themselves. We try to love them when they can't love themselves."

"How do people hear about it?"

"Folks hear about it and they come."

"In light of the recent arrests, do you ever worry that dangerous criminals will think of it as some sort of haven or sanctuary where they can repay their debt to society in lieu of going to prison? A sort of validation scheme that actually exacerbates crime?"

How would that word *exacerbate* go over in a children's book?

"I don't worry about that, no," said Helen. Everything my wife said I imagined reading in tomorrow's newspaper.

"Did you welcome The Doctor into the Sad Kitchen?"

"Dominic came to us on the night of his arrest, but I didn't get to speak with him."

"He had never come before that night?"

"Not to my knowledge. I never got the

chance to meet Dominic." Helen seemed to be going out of her way to say that word, *Dominic.* I wanted to tell her to watch her language.

"Would you have welcomed Dr. Spencer into the Sad Kitchen if you had met him?"

"Of course. All are welcome. I would have loved to talk with Dominic."

Melinda's face seemed to twitch. "Mrs. Sampson, since you've sort of made sympathy and forgiveness your claim to fame, tell me, do you believe that Dominic Spencer should go to prison for his crimes?"

"I wish I could give a nice, sexy snippet for your story, but my job is to love. I apologize if that is bland."

"It isn't bland, but it seems a little easy and sentimental, Mrs. Sampson. It's a cop-out and it completely ignores justice."

"I really wish I could give you a sexy snippet. I sure do."

Now Melinda studied my wife's face with much diligence. She looked like she wanted to reach out and touch it. "Mrs. Sampson," said Melinda, "what would you say in response to the claim that you are nothing more than a sociopathic, masochistic monomaniac, or some kind of—of—of recreant agent provocateur camouflaged by a grandmotherly facade?"

A small laugh from my Helen. "I would ask to borrow a thesaurus," she said and then, for some reason, both faces turned toward me, as if I would produce a thesaurus. But I had forgotten that I wasn't a just a fly on the wall. I must have looked quite stupid and unprepared, because they looked back to one another, and now came a sneaky little twist by Melinda, switching from one headline to another. "Last question for the time being, Mrs. Sampson. I promise this will be my final attempt to get you to say something you'll regret. Ready? Do you think one year is enough prison time for raping a young girl?"

"It's difficult for me to imagine spending even one night in prison away from my Bubba," said my sweet Helen. "A year sounds just awful."

Then the duality of their special rapport finally and completely exposed itself as Melinda took a deep breath and said, "I'm sorry for asking you these tough questions so rapid fire. It's my job."

What a shocking comment. I nearly sat down on the floor.

"That's okay," said Helen.

"When you read the editorial in tomorrow's

paper, my sympathy won't come through. But it's there. I promise."

"I've been warned," said Helen.

"The truth is," said Melinda, "that I have heard about the Sad Kitchen. Oh sure, I've heard about it through the various professional channels that led me here, but I've also *heard* about it the way folks hear about it."

"What did you think?" said Helen.

"I thought it sounded intriguing and I would like to come by sometime just to see how it works."

"I hope you will."

"Let me finish. I thought it sounded intriguing and I would like to come by sometime, but it won't sound that way when you read the editorial I'm going to write." Now Melinda, the young woman I had mistaken for a tough-cookie, began to sniffle just a little. "I don't know what to tell you. I'm sorry. It is unbelievably complicated. This life is just booby-trapped. You sound like such a good, kind lady, but if I'm being honest I've already written the editorial. And if I'm being *perfectly* honest, the editorial has already been signed-off on by my boss. He just needed me to come here to fill in a few quotes."

"A few snippets," said Helen, looking pleased with herself.

"Oh, what am I doing?" lamented poor Melinda. "Why am I saying these things? Ugh, this is so awful."

I wanted to scream because I didn't understand, and I was terrified. But I was too dumbfounded to rediscover the use of my tongue. It was the most complicated conversation I had ever witnessed. Soon Helen was ushering the young woman to the door. She had her hand on the young woman's back and my tongue lay stupidly inside the hole in my face.

I tried to pick up their coffee mugs, but my hands were too shaky. Would you believe me if I said my wife has never seemed more powerful than she did that morning talking to the reporter in our kitchenette? *Powerful* is the only word to describe it, and the reason I was incapable of speech that morning, the reason my hands were so shaky, was out of sheer terror of this woman whom I love.

When she returned after having seen the young woman off, I had the urge to say, "Why do you refuse to defend yourself, you bat-shit, crazy-assed woman? Do you not realize how damn, flat-out cowardly that was?" but my tongue gave me the power to say, "Are you ever afraid of anything?" and she said, "Oh gosh, all the time, Bubba," while she picked up the coffee mugs with the steadiest hands.

CHAPTER FIVE

The next morning Melinda's editorial was published with the headline, "A Haven for Dangerous Criminals."

There was a picture of Jack's Diner (during the daytime) and then the mug shots of Dominic Spencer and Vern and Kurt and Janice and Mike.

"Do you want me to read it to you?" I said on the car ride home.

"That's okay. I think I'd rather not know."

The editorial called Helen a "compulsive and indiscriminate sympathizer, a monomaniac, and a provocateur who fails to think strategically and neglects to understand that a failure to account for human failings is, in and of itself, a deep moral failure."

Another bit said: "To believe that blind kindness is a fundamentally sound response to any situation is, in and of itself, nothing less than the gravest form of unkindness, all the more dangerous for the fact that it is masked behind a charismatic smile."

Another: "What is at stake here is the difference between evil and corruption. Evil is easy to understand, even by its agent. If you were to ask, for example, the Doctor [Dominic Spencer] himself, whether sodomizing anesthetized patients is evil, he would agree: yes, it is evil. But if you were to ask Mrs. Sampson, in a similar vein, whether harboring and comforting these degraded categories of criminals is evil, she would deny it as such. *This* is corruption. And the difference between evil and corruption is of ultimate significance here. If you, dear reader, don't believe me, then consider the extreme. If you were to ask Hitler in 1940 whether his movement to exterminate entire races was 'evil,' he would have said, without the bat of a lash, no. Corruption is more dangerous than evil because it is willfully blind and blindly charismatic. Mrs. Sampson is a charismatic woman, but she is willfully blind, and her blindness is emblematic of—dare I say central to?—a greater problem of leniency in our society toward criminals, especially criminals of a violent inclination.

"I will leave you with this: if you still disagree with the power of corruption, consider the extreme nature of my words here. The fundamental power of corruption is founded in its ability to make anything that contradicts it seem extreme or over-reactionary or whiney or, more broadly, uncharismatic. I urge you, fellow citizens, to consider what is at stake here. We *have* a blind spot. We *are* corrupt. Rape and thievery and violence *are* tolerated in this society. Corruption has the power to normalize evil, and evil *has* been normalized. Let us be awakened. Let us grind our teeth against the smiling face of corruption. Let us be the resistance."

I didn't know what to say, and sometimes I still don't. The whole time I read the darn thing, I believed the emotion I was experiencing was pure anger. But then a tear dripped from my nose. It was more complicated than anger, I guess. The dot of my tear smeared the newsprint to gray. Helen patted my thigh and drove.

The protests began that night. When Helen and I arrived downtown, they had already set up a medium-sized spotlight under and around which there was a healthy smattering of about 50 people, 70. Also there were some police officers with crossed arms hanging around, and two news vans. The signs the protestors held ranged from things like, "You can't hide anymore!" to "This city protects rapists!" to "Don't legalize rape!" to "Castrate rapists!"

Helen and I sat in the car in the alley at a distance and watched for quite a while, silent. I didn't dare say anything because, whatever I would have said, it would have been foul. But Helen must have known what was going on inside my head because she said, "It's only some folks with strong feelings."

"What should we do?"

"Our job is to love—"

"That's not what I mean. I mean what should we do right *now*? I'm talking about practicalities here, Helen. Poor Jack is in there right now closing Jack's Diner for the evening. Soon he will have to leave and walk through that mess. Anything could happen."

"I'll go talk to Jack."

"No," I said. "Let me go. I don't want those news vans seeing your face."

"Do I look that bad, Bubba?" said Helen, checking her face in the rearview mirror.

I had to give this comment some rigorous contemplation before it even registered in my brain: a joke. Helen had made a little joke.

I'm all for using humor to declaw a ferocious situation, but in God's name, this moment was too awful even for the power of humor. An anger seized me and grew tighter and tighter until, at the very moment before a vein somewhere deep inside me was going to rupture, a tranquil realization came over me: this woman has lost her God-forsaken mind. Based on her performance last night during the interview in the kitchenette, and now this comedy act, it was the simplest conclusion. I was dealing with a veritable lunatic.

It had never dawned on me until this moment, but now it was totalizing: people *do* lose their minds in stressful situations as a sort of defense mechanism. It does happen, especially to folks our age. And now it was happening to my Helen.

I needed to rub my temples for a while. "Do me a favor, Helen" I said after a nice massage of my frontal lobe. "Can you please say *one* thing to prove to me that you haven't gone totally looney? Any old thing will do, as long as it sounds like something a sane person would say. Even if you would just imitate a sane person for a moment, it would be helpful. I need this. I'm not being a jokester right now. I just need to hear one logical, rational thing come out of your face. Something that I can use to draw even a faint comparison between my wife and a relatively grounded individual."

After she studied my eyes for a while her lips seemed to resign into a smile, as if it were her natural condition. "I'm angry too, Bubba," she said and patted my thigh. "Angry and afraid."

My wife parked the car and together we made way toward the Sad Kitchen. Going past the protestors, we must have looked like folks trying to escape a cold gust of wind. We turned up our collars and hunched into ourselves and scurried along. Only once did I look the protestors in the face and now, as I try to remember what I saw, I cannot recall any particulars. Instead my memory produces a single snapshot of a solitary creature whose face is warped with torment, as if it were dealing with a painful and unruly bowel movement.

Then we stepped inside the womb that is the Sad Kitchen and all was quiet and very warm.

The moment Helen crosses the threshold in the evening, Jack's Diner completes its nightly transition to the Sad Kitchen.

That night the Sad Kitchen was entirely empty but for one soul: at the counter, there sat Jack himself, hunched over a can of light beer.

"Well here we are," said Jack.

"I'm so sorry, Jack," said my wife.

"Would you all like a light beer?" said Jack.

"This is my fault," said Helen.

"Yes," I said. "I'll take a light beer."

"Good!" said Jack and slapped the counter a little bit and Helen jumped in her shoes. Jack went around the counter and got a beer out of a grocery bag and cracked it and handed it over.

"Are you sure you won't join us?" he said to Helen.

"Why don't you have one?" I said, feeling suddenly good, like a young man.

"Well, maybe one," said Helen.

Jack grabbed her a light beer and told her to have a seat at the counter. "You sit there and have yourself a light beer and quit that yammering about being sorry. It toxifies the atmosphere."

I don't know whether I'd ever seen Helen take a seat at the counter of the Sad Kitchen. It looked very unnatural. "Now," said Jack, "tell me you're not sorry before God packs his bag and starts limping off into eternity."

I like Jack. Old Jack has always impressed me. I couldn't help but feel that my display back in the car was partially to blame for Helen's sudden self-doubt. Jack had a nice third-person perspective, and now he was using it to fix things. Helen took a cute, tentative nip of her beer. "Well I'm just sorry how things have turned out for you, Jack."

"Nope, nope, nope!" said Jack. "I'm a part of this. You take another sip of that light beer and tell me how it really is."

Helen took a good nip. "Fine then. I'm not sorry, darn you," she said and grinned.

"Good!" said Jack. "Again!"

She took another good nip and then hiccupped. "I'm not sorry, darn you!"

"Again!" said both Jack and I now.

Helen raised her light beer, "I'm not sorry, boys!"

We sat at the counter, three in a row with Helen in the middle, having our light beers and waiting, although it wasn't clear specifically what we were waiting for. It could have been said that we were just buying time while Jack gathered the courage to brave the protestors. It could also have been said that we were waiting for our first customer of the night to arrive, but because of the situation outside no customers were forthcoming.

In truth I think we were waiting for something more complicated than we could have put our collective finger on, and it went unspoken because it would have been too complicated to speak it. Because what happened as we "waited," was that, by and by, Helen and Jack began to reminisce about their dead son, the shortstop, while I sat and learned fascinating information.

First, Jack compared his situation (being stuck in the Sad Kitchen and not wanting to face the hard reality waiting outside the door in the alleyway) with a little anecdote about their son from when he was just a toddler. "I remember one time I was showing him how to play with a toy truck in a sandbox somewhere or other, and all of a sudden the kid started trying to open the little, miniature door! 'What are you doin, bud?'

I asked him real calm. '*In!*' he said, 'I want to get in!' He wanted to get in the little truck! How do you explain to a human being that they can't get inside of a toy truck that was no bigger than the palm of his hand? That kid must have cried for an hour!"

Jack's story was some much-needed lightheartedness, but by far the most interesting tidbit of the conversation came a little later, from Helen.

"He came up with a theory one day," said Helen after she and Jack had been reminiscing for a good while. "He was a real thinker, that boy—he was like you that way, Bubba," she continued, leaving me shocked and flattered and convinced that it was my duty and obligation to write this ridiculous book. "And one of his best theories of all times was that folks have a God-given right to believe that anything and everything is a miracle. I still remember when he came home from school—he must have been in fourth or fifth grade, back when I was still his favorite person in the world—and he came home one day and told me that he had been getting some grief from his friends for his new theory. I asked him what the theory was, and he told it to me, plain as can be: '*Everything* is a miracle, Mamma.' But if you could have seen the wonder in the eyes of this child that I had already come to believe was a miracle incarnate, you would see that there was no good reason to doubt him. All of reality seemed to wink at me and for a small moment he no longer bothered to hide what he truly was: a child of God. Oh, I sound so silly. Let me try to put it another way. It was as if a set of blinds were quickly pulled—a set of blinds that I didn't even know were there in the first place!—and all of a sudden I could see beyond my son's eyes and into a big, beautiful new place. It felt like a very beautiful place, Bubba," she said, suddenly turning to me, although her eyes were still there and were very serious. They hadn't been opened like blinds.

"Anywho," she said, "that was the only time we ever spoke of it—his special little theory. For all I know, he had forgotten all about it by the time of his death, but it sure stuck with me. I think in his own special way he was preparing me for his death to come. Of course, in those days, I was pretty lukewarm about things, but I just couldn't forget that special little moment and I couldn't shake that darn theory! It seems so simple now, but I was a single mother working at a dry cleaner and I guess I was always waiting

for the universe to give me some type of a wink
or a sad embrace or a friendly smile. After that,
everyone and everything I saw, big or small,
good or bad, no matter, I tried my darnedest
to see it just that way: a miracle. Something
to be thankful for. A wink or a sad embrace
or a friendly smile from God. And to this day
the only thing that ever prevents it is my own
doggone cynicism. Now, that's all I'll say on the
matter before I start sounding silly."

I waited for either Jack or myself to say, "*Silly*
just left the building and is skipping naked
down Broad Street singing gospel hymns," but,
miraculously, neither of us did. Instead, we let
Helen's little anecdote stretch its achy limbs
in the space of the Sad Kitchen, and it was
very nice for a while, but, as these things go, I
eventually felt the dull weight of my compulsive
need to ask a question: the question that is
really just a version of all questions that have
ever been asked. All of a sudden I found my
stupid, simple self face-to-face with eternity.
How quickly that could happen! One moment I
was listening to a little story, and the next thing
I knew I was ready to challenge my wife and her

God and even my very existence. *Don't ask it, don't ask it, don't ask it,* I was telling myself, very urgent.

I was able to resist, but it didn't matter. The special moment was dead.

The question, of course, was going to be: "Why would God let your son be brutally murdered at such a young age? How is *that* a miracle, you crazy, crazy, bat-brained woman?"

It must have been a few hours later—around 9 or 10 p.m.—that we heard a sudden yelping, moaning sound behind us. We all three turned. It hadn't actually been a yelp, of course, but only the front door opening and delivering the sound of the protestors outside. Jack, Helen, and I had been reminiscing for so long that we had forgotten that the door existed. Then the door shut against the sound of the protestors and the womb of silence once again held us, but now we were four instead of three.

Standing just inside the door was Melinda, the young woman who had come to our apartment, sat in our kitchenette, sipped our coffee, and then published the awful editorial about my wife. When I saw her standing there, I said to myself, *Right, this makes perfect sense*, but I couldn't decipher whether I was being sarcastic with myself or honest-to-God.

"I didn't come for a meal and a ticket," she said. "I just came to see how this place works."

"Like any good reporter would," said my wife, smiling at the young woman who looked lost. Little did any of us know, Melinda hadn't just stepped over the threshold of our front door, but she had also stepped over a threshold of her life and into a vast unknown. It's no wonder the poor girl looked lost and alone.

My wife went and greeted Melinda and brought her into the Sad Kitchen and introduced her to Jack. I watched Jack's face perform some impressive acrobatics as he came first to the realization that this was the woman who had written the libelous drivel of an editorial and, second, that he was going to have to be welcoming and kind to the young woman because Helen wouldn't tolerate anything less.

Don't worry, Jack, I was right there with you, pal. I was positively teeming with the most creative array of spiteful comments. But "Aren't we glad to see you," is what came out of my mouth.

"Bubba why don't you go put on some coffee for Melinda here?" said Helen.

"None for me, thank you," said Melinda.

"She doesn't want any," I said to Helen.

"Won't you put on some coffee, Bubba? A nice big, fresh pot."

"Who the heck for?" I tried to say politely.

"Me," said Helen. "Do it for me."

"You're going to drink an entire pot of coffee on your own?" I said.

"Yes," said Helen, quite snooty.

Helen has a way of making you feel like an ornery teenager if you argue with her. I decided to shut up and make a pot of coffee before my dignity was gone in front of Melinda.

"Let me show you around," said Helen to Melinda.

"As you can see we are not very busy this evening," said Jack, a little sarcastic, and I'm afraid I scoffed along with him.

"Ignore them," said Helen. "They get ornery when they are bored. Come on back and I'll show you the kitchen."

Melinda followed Helen through the bat-wing doors. Jack and I hung back and did not talk. This was normal for Jack and me. Whenever we were alone, we did not speak to one another. It was part of our manly rapport.

While the coffee was perking, I decided I would go check on Helen and Melinda. But when I approached the bat-wing door, a tender silence stayed me. Against this silence, as if to check for a heartbeat, I placed my ear.

"You terrify me, Miss Helen," said Melinda.

"It must be my purple turtleneck," said my wife.

"Please don't be coy right now. Please don't. I don't understand what's going on and I'm terrified by you and everything you stand for. Frankly, I don't understand why I respect you at all. And I don't understand why I'm here right now. Sure, you are kind and sweet in person, but when I think about the bigger picture, you strike me as insincere and self-righteous and evil and brainwashed and a little creepy, too. On paper, I should hate you."

"You already did hate me on paper," said my wife.

"You delude evil people into believing that they are good, but you trick perfectly good people into hating themselves. Why do I hate myself right now? Tell me, Miss Helen. Please, I need to understand. Please, just explain it to me so I can understand what I'm dealing with."

"I'm not hiding anything. Everything you see is just how it is."

"Don't say that. That is infuriating and a cop-out and you know it! Now, explain it to me!"

"Well, let me see here," said my wife, bumbling a little. "Why don't you try this on? I'm afraid this is the only explanation there is."

Unable to help myself, I peeked over the bat-wing doors and glimpsed my wife handing Melinda one of our aprons. Melinda was sitting on the stove range with her face in her hands in the shape of a person totally distraught. I tried to get a better view—to see whether Melinda would take the apron—but in my attempt, I stumbled into the bat-wing doors. Helen said, "Hi Bubba."

"Uh," I stammered. "The coffee is perking."

"Thanks Bubba. We will be out in a few minutes."

I turned and went back to my not-conversation with Jack. We had some important things to not talk about.

A few minutes later, Helen came through the bat-wing doors followed by Melinda. Melinda was wearing the apron Helen had given her. I tried to determine whether the situation called for a sly comment such as, "Ain't exactly a ballgown, is it?" or "That sure goes nice with your manicure," but decided to swallow my wit. Helen pulled a roller cart out of a closet and instructed me to place the 50-cupper coffee urn on the cart. A scheme was being set in motion: Helen placed a sleeve of paper cups on the roller cart and gave Melinda authority over all of it. Her task was to bring the cart outside to provide coffee for all the folks protesting in the alleyway.

While Melinda went outside, Helen smiled primly at Jack and me and then headed back into the kitchen. Jack's and my options were few: we sat looking at our hands.

After a while, Melinda came back inside and Helen made her a plate of eggs and hash browns and she sat at the end of the counter poking at it and moving it around.

"Did they enjoy the coffee?" called Jack down the counter in a cruel voice.

"Well anyway, they are drinking it," said Melinda to her plate of food.

"Good," said Helen.

"I told them that I was here doing some investigative work," said Melinda. "I told them they have every right to be angry."

"That's okay," said Helen. "In a lot of ways that's all truthful. Now, just enjoy that plate of food."

The next night the size of the protestors was cut in half. But the most passionate folks were still out there hollering away, and we didn't have any Sad Kitchen customers. Melinda arrived around 10 p.m.

Jack had had enough. Upon the sight of Melinda for the second consecutive night, old Jack drummed his fingers on the counter, got up, and left the Sad Kitchen. He was ready to brave the protestors, I guess. "Bubba, Helen, I will see you tomorrow."

I almost followed Jack out. In fact, half of me did follow him—the angry part. I was very pleasant with Melinda the rest of the night. Maybe my hostile feelings toward Melinda had all been part of a put-on to impress Jack. Who knows? "You just let me know if you need more coffee out there," I said to Melinda with the voice of a peace offering.

"You just let me know if you ever need a proper lesson in how to change the oil in your automobile," she said, completely rounding out her personality in a wonderful way. *Oh*, I said to myself, smiling like an old fool I'm sure, *this is the real Melinda. Now I get it.*

My wife has always given off a slight rosy odor when she sleeps. Maybe it is a scent of secret perfume or maybe it is something womanly which I should not be speculating over in a place like this. When I lift the covers of our bed, the smell fills my nostrils and I start to consider new aspects of my life. One day during the time of the protests, my wife and I were lying in bed and the smell went quickly to my thoughts and I had no choice but to wake up my wife. "Helen...psst...hey lady."

"Hi Bubba."

"Helen, I just realized something. I've never really believed Vern's story. The one about the tree growing up through his prison cell."

"Well that's okay," she said, groggy and sleepy. "It's only natural to be a little suspicious."

"Do you believe his story, Helen?"

"What's this about all of a sudden, Bubba?" She was coming awake and the rosy odor was gone.

"All of a sudden it's got me a little guilty. It's not so much that I'm suspicious, because like you said it's only natural, but it's the *reason* I'm suspicious that has me bothered. I'm only now realizing the *reason*."

She rolled over and looked me in the eye so that I was nervous. "Well, what's the reason?"

"I think the reason I'm so suspicious is that I have it in my mind that a miraculous thing like that wouldn't happen to a person like Vern. If it were someone else—say an innocent man— I'd have no trouble believing it. But since it's Vern…geesh, now that I say it aloud it sounds just awful."

"Might be you should say a little prayer," she said rubbing my shoulder. "Might be you just need to sort through some doubts, Bubba."

So I attempted a little prayer. I tried to make it a good and special prayer, but I wound up in a familiar place. "God, who are you? Amen."

The next night the protestors were only a tenth as large as the first night. I guess the others had lives and schedules that were not conducive to nocturnal protesting, and thus they were starting to get worn down after three nights. Some Sad Kitchen customers were returning, and Jack seemed to be in a better mood about Melinda's presence. Fireman John Rogers was there that night, and Valli, and a few of the newer and unnamed (unfortunately) folks who joined us later on with the 250-batch of Vern's book.

In total there were fewer than ten protestors left outside, and Helen sent Melinda to invite them inside to eat with our smattering of customers. While Melinda was out in the alley delivering our peace offering, we waited inside, quite eager. I must admit that I was beginning to feel a little sentimental. An image of impending peace and warmth and coziness flooded me with a giddiness, and out gushed this statement: "That Melinda is a good kid," I said to my wife.

"We're lucky to have her, Bubba," said my wife, quiet and composed. "We're getting older and older."

"I don't know, I'm feeling renewed! My back doesn't hurt anymore! This peace offering is going to work wonders! We're going to get through this just fine. God is on our side."

Helen gave a small laugh.

"Are you not feeling renewed, Helen?"

"I'm feeling okay," said Helen, and before I could pick at her any further, Melinda reentered the Sad Kitchen with three protestors.

"Welcome," said my wife. "Where are all the others?" she said.

One of the protestors spat a good-sized wad on the floor. "This is phony!" he said to my wife and Melinda.

"This is just a token peace offering to get us out of your goddamn hair! What a racket!" said another.

"You are essentially attacking us with your passive-aggressive moral superiority," said a third. "It's just degrading!" He looked around for something to punch but there was nothing very convenient.

Now Fireman John Rogers—the man who never speaks—stood from his booth and walked over to the protestors. "THIS IS A FRIENDLY PLACE!" he screamed right in the third protestor's face, lodging everyone's breath in their throats like a ping pong ball.

At this, Valli was so spooked she became

hysterical. She began to scream unintelligible expletives at my wife and they were horrible. The sound she delivered was prehistoric, like a pterodactyl screaming as it gets hit by a bolt of primeval lightning. I had been heading over to restrain Fireman John Rogers who was scowling and bulking at the protestors, but now I redirected my attention to Valli. I restrained her from behind, full nelson, and simultaneously attempted to cover her mouth out of fear that her voice itself would pierce my poor wife's old and tired heart. I felt like an orderly in a psychiatric unit.

While I restrained Valli, I noticed my wife's face. In my wife's face I saw fear.

Jack and a few others went over to try to defuse Fireman John Rogers. Meanwhile, Melinda tried to wedge herself between John Rogers and the protestors. In my arms, Valli's body seemed to be filled with lightning, and she screamed and screamed. The protestors went silent as the situation begged to be gawked at. Welcome, friends, to the epitome of the Sad Kitchen.

On the drive home that morning, my wife's face was still fearful, as if it had been petrified by Valli's prehistoric screaming. I sat there trying to figure out what to say. But my wife spoke first. Of all the things in the world that could have come out of her fearful face in a situation like that, the thing that came out of it was this: "I've been having the runs, Bubba."

What was I supposed to do with that? "Might be you've got a little bug," I said, feeling exhausted.

"I've been having them for a while now. Well, a long while, actually. And it's a little bloody, too."

"Oh," I probably said.

"I scheduled a doctor's appointment for next week," I think she said, and her casual tone-of-voice irritated me.

"Oh," I probably said again. I'll bet my face was now just as fearful as my wife's.

CHAPTER SIX

The protesters did not come anymore. They did not send us a letter to inform us that their protest was thereby concluded.

Our protest is hereby concluded. Carry on.

Nothing like that.

Many times I had assumed the Sad Kitchen was dead and buried. This was once again what I assumed after the escapades of John Rogers and Valli in front of the protestors. But it was springtime now, and as surely as spring follows winter, as surely as the drunk man stumbles home and falls face-first and cross-eyed into his cold mattress, we sustained. Slowly the regulars returned, and more and more new folks simply staggered in. Karen the lawyer, one of our earliest customers, was back with us.

"Do you believe this?" I said one night filling her cup, sad, while every seat in the joint was filled. "I thought we were dead and buried."

"Maybe we are dead and buried, Bubba," she said smirking a sneaky lawyer smirk. "Maybe this is what dead and buried looks like."

"Is that what passes for decent lawyer humor these days?"

"All I know is I used to think Purgatory would be set in a courtroom where we are all just a bunch of defendants. But God willing, it will be more like this place."

"Alright, take it easy, lady."

"Think about it, Bubba. Which would you rather be subjected to? In a courtroom, the truth is a matter of consensus, but in here, it's just the opposite. In here, consensus is a matter of *truth*."

"I'm going to need another cup of coffee, a calculator, and a telescope before I can go any further with this sort of talk."

Karen laughed, sweet and sympathetic of my simple mind. By the end of that month we would have at least 120 customers per night.

It is possible that this was always just a story about a polyp in my wife's large intestine, even from the very beginning. When I was rambling on about Vern's children's book, I could have been discussing the little polyp's youth and development into an angry, malignant tumor. When I was explaining how she taught me to use prayer to discover the stillness inside of me, her insides were simultaneously being ravished. When I was discussing the terrible 11 o'clock news disaster, I could just as easily have been talking about all the metastases to her liver and lungs. This book was always growing further and further from childhood, and I won't rule out the possibility that it did so in order to make room for words like *colonoscopy* and *malignant* and *metastasis*.

Watching her walk into the doctor's office from the waiting room I wondered if she looked skinnier. But I lacked a frame of reference, which is to say I was incapable of seeing her as a person, was only capable of seeing my entire life. This reminds me of a fellow, Judson, on my ward in prison who had a little daughter with cancer of the blood. He told me one time that good health is a window, but sickness is a mirror. At the time I hadn't a clue what old

125

Judson was talking about. But it has stuck with me all these years.

When she came out of the doctor's office, my wife's face was just a cloudy image of her knelt in prayer and it caused me to stand up. "What did they tell you?" I said.

"They said to eat a toast-based diet and that I need to have a colonoscopy."

"I can help with the toast-based diet," I said automatically. "But not the other."

When Helen laughed, her face came back, and it occurred to me that I had made a joke.

"They said I'll need someone to drive me to the colonoscopy," said my wife on the drive home patting my thigh. "You can help with that too."

"Are we going to go on pretending that I'm going to be useful in a situation like this?" I asked.

"Let's don't call it a situation. Let's don't call it a *this*, how about."

"What should we call it? You seem to have all the answers. You tell me what to call it."

"Let's don't call it an *it*, either," she said, almost pleased with herself.

"Well then what the hell!" I said. "What the hell!"

"It just *is*," she said, very coy.

I wasn't sure whether we were arguing or renewing our marital vows. "Are you being prim with me, woman?" I said out of genuine curiosity, I think.

"Oh Bubba."

If I give the impression that I gave a damn about anything other than my wife's bowels those days, it is a false one. Her bowels composed the most extraordinary nightmare. They were somewhere wet and haunted and yet warm and womblike for me to reside. Their endless shifting and churning became a terrible opera in my head.

The newest rebirth of the Sad Kitchen was just something to fiddle with as we waited to have the colonoscopy and then afterward, once we knew.

Sometimes these days I would be doing my duties at the Sad Kitchen and it would occur to me to pat my eyes to see if my fingertips would come away with tears.

"Is your eye okay?" said some customer, any old customer.

"Is there something wrong with my eye?" I said.

"Hey, take it easy, bub. I was only asking because you keep touching it."

"How about you let me worry about my eye and I'll let you worry about yours."

"Isn't that from the Bible?" said another customer down the counter.

"That would make great sense because I pulled it right out of my ass. Sorry, I didn't mean that."

"Bubba, what's going on, bud?"

"Oh hell," I said. That was just the way of things nowadays.

Melinda was wonderful nowadays because she became a Sad Kitchen rover who helped my wife with the cooking and helped me with the serving and the camaraderie. She was a very dynamic lady. Whether she discerned that something was awry with my wife's large intestine, I do not know.

"Don't you ever get tired, girly?" I said, knowing full well she wouldn't like that word, *girly.*

"Why would I get tired? I am young and

128

vivacious. You're the old bag of bones with a bum back."

"I'm not the one with a day job though." I used a cruel voice to say *day job*.

"Eh. I quit that."

"Say you did?"

"Well kind of," she said, continuing to rove about her duties in order to prove that I didn't deserve her full attention. "One of those protestors took a picture of me helping out around here and brought it to my boss as blackmail. My boss was going to fire me anyway. Or at least demote me."

Wow. I thought. *Whatever Helen's got, this gal has it too.* "Oh," was probably my response.

"Now put those old bones back to work," said Melinda.

She was a good kid, growing younger every night.

One day in bed my wife had told me all about Melinda's initial consternation with the Sad Kitchen. In short, Melinda didn't appreciate how Vern had become the focus of a story of which he was not the true center.

"What does she think is the true center?" I asked my wife.

"Izzy and her son," said my wife.

"Oh," I must have said.

"And you know what? She's exactly right, too."

"Well it was never our intention to make this a story about Vern." I said. "It was never our intention to make this a story at all! It just happened that way—"

"Doesn't matter, Bubba. It just doesn't matter."

"Okay," I said, feeling a little scolded. "Well, what do we do about it?"

"Well, Melinda has taken it upon herself to try to reach out to Izzy. But it's delicate."

The magnitude of my wife's small whispers gripped a ripcord around my ribs and yanked. "Is there anything I should be doing?"

"Prayer," said my wife, rolling over in bed. "God is a gathering force, Bubba. Between His love and His mercy, He gathers us."

I tried a little prayer, but my wife was soon asleep, and I was left alone inside the trembling darkness of her bowels.

As we were getting more and more customers per night, Karen the lawyer arrived early one evening to discuss something with my wife and me. Jack had just left for the night and Melinda was yet to arrive, so it was only the three of us in the Sad Kitchen.

Karen was wearing jeans and a sweatshirt. I'd never seen her in anything but her two-piece lawyer's suit and high heels. She seemed nervous.

"I didn't know you owned regular human clothes," I said a little sarcastically to Karen. "You look like the doggone salt of the earth."

"What is it, hun?" said Helen to Karen and slapped the back of my head a little.

Karen swallowed. "Helen, Bubba, I would like to hereby devote the entirety of my time, talent, and treasure to the Sad Kitchen."

"Karen, you're one of our longest-lasting customers," said my wife. "You don't need to do anything more—"

"This is important," said Karen. "We are growing and growing. You two could use some help around here and God knows the kind of financial imposition we are on poor Jack. I'm a single woman in my forties and I'm swimming in my own savings. Let me do this. Just let me."

"What's your end game here, woman?" I blurted. "You've got a job. You've got a life.

Don't do this. Who knows how much longer we are for this world."

"The Sad Kitchen will never die," said Karen, a little too sheepish even to meet our eyes. "No offense, but it's bigger than the two of you. It's bigger than any of us, than all of us put together. Can't you see that it is sustained by its own failings, which are us?"

Helen gave Karen a good hug and they were weepy together. "Miss Helen, you feel thin! Are you doing okay, baby girl?"

Worse than ever, I needed to go sit down in a corner by myself.

That night, as if Karen were prophetic, the Sad Kitchen had, for the first time ever, a line of folks reaching out the door and curling into the alleyway where only a few weeks earlier the protestors had been. Karen became our greeter and coordinator and hostess. She looked happy and just-right in her sweatshirt and jeans, and the clipboard she held gave her as much authority as her two-piece suit ever had. Melinda looked happy too in her duty as rover. The bat-wing doors seemed to automatically open for her when she gave them a good hard look of determination.

I lost count at approximately 200 new faces that night. I wondered what Vern would think about all this. An overwhelmed feeling poured over me: for a brief moment I suddenly cared about everything again. Then I remembered my wife's bowels and I cared about nothing. How liberating. I poured some coffee and stared, poured some coffee and stared.

The night before the day of the colonoscopy was upon us. Over the course of the night, Helen was supposed to drink a gallon of special liquid that would "clear you out." At times these days it felt like my true duty in all of this was to enact just the right amount of stupidity so that we could go on pretending a little longer that my wife wasn't losing her dignity in front of my very eyes. Saying *clear you out* was a very effective form of stupidity.

As we were about to leave for the night, Helen wore her winter coat (even though it was springtime) and she held her big gallon of liquid to her chest like a little girl. She looked just like a little girl.

"Why are you looking at me like that, Bubba?"

"No reason. Say, can we just pretend that I said, 'Why don't you take the night off from the Sad Kitchen,' without me actually having to say it since I know you won't hear me anyhow?"

She laughed and casually destroyed me. "Sure, Sweetheart."

That night at the Sad Kitchen, a new development: the line out the door and into the alleyway was longer than ever and Karen came inside with her clipboard reporting that folks were offering to take tickets without even receiving a meal and some coffee in exchange. "They just want a ticket," she told me.

"That defeats the whole purpose!" I exclaimed, easily exercised these days.

"But if they're offering, shouldn't we let them? The tickets are the whole point."

I just shook my head. "I don't know. Go ask my wife."

But Karen came back a few minutes later. "Um, Bubba. I can't find Helen. Melinda says she hasn't seen her in over twenty minutes."

Then I remembered that tonight was Helen's night to be cleared out.

There is a little restroom back in the kitchen and I knocked with one knuckle and put my cheek against it. "Helen, it's Bubba."

"Hi, Bubba," came the small reply.

"Are you okay in there?"

No reply and no reply and then I heard the lock give.

"Do you want me to enter?"

"Come in, Bubba."

This story has already gotten far enough from childhood, so I'll just tell you what I found when I entered. My wife was on the toilet hugging her jug of liquid and some of her mess was on the floor and on her pants and it was bloody, and my wife was on the other side of a veil of tears.

"This is where we're at, Bubba," she said, and then disappeared behind her veil.

"Okay," I said. "Alright."

"But it's okay, Bubba," said my wife, veiled. "It will be alright."

"I will go get some aprons so we can wrap you up and get you out of here."

"You don't need to do that. No, it's going to be alright. No, you don't need to do that," said my wife, strangely at peace behind her veil. I didn't trust this peacefulness about her.

Melinda found me as I searched for some extra aprons. "Is everything okay with Helen, Bubba?"

"I don't know how to explain it."

"Well, I'm not asking you to explain it, you goon…" she said, still lighthearted.

"NO!" I screamed at her face. "EVERYTHING IS NOT ALRIGHT WITH HELEN!"

"Let me help. Bubba, just let me."

She followed me back to the bathroom.

"Oh you don't need to be dealing with this, Sweetie," Helen said to Melinda as I held up some aprons for my wife to use as a gown.

"Miss Helen," said Melinda, astonished.

"It's okay," said Helen. "I'm alright."

Melinda must have been able to decipher that Helen was in a state of shock because now she looked me in the eye and spoke to me as if Helen were not even present: "I will clean this up. You can take her out. Let me worry about this."

"It's okay, Sweetie," said my wife to Melinda from a different planet.

"I know, Miss Helen. I know."

She was all wrapped up in aprons and with one arm I was attempting to usher her through the Sad Kitchen as inconspicuously as possible while holding her jug of liquid with my other. It worked for a while, until we got to the crowded doorway and then outside where the line of folks was waiting to enter. "Is that Miss Helen?" came some mutters.

And, "Hi, Miss Helen!"

"That's her, alright!"

"Miss Helen, pray for me!"

"Miss Helen, you rock my world!"

My wife kept attempting to pull away from me to talk with these folks, but I had to usher her along. "We'll be right back, damnit!" I lied over my shoulder.

"We'll be right back!" my wife repeated, very eager to please.

We didn't sleep that night because my wife was mostly in the bathroom and I was mostly staring at the darkness of our bedroom and by the morning my wife's strange state of shock had worn off and she grew very quiet.

The moment seemed to require me to act like a husband, which is a concept that has always puzzled me. But I thought I'd figured it out when, as I drank a cup of coffee at our little table in the kitchenette and looked at her, I said, "Listen, Helen, you don't need to be embarrassed."

"Embarrassed about what, Bubba?"

"Well…you know…about the scene in the bathroom last evening."

"Why should I be embarrassed? That was just me opening up to you. I was just showing you my insides."

She intended this as stroke of grotesque humor, but I didn't let myself laugh. Instead, I studied her eyes. In her eyes, I saw a mirror. In the mirror of her eyes she laid bare something that I had hidden from myself. The truth was I had only brought up the issue of "embarrassment" because I was embarrassed on my own behalf because of her, embarrassed to be known as a man whose wife shits on the floor, embarrassed that I was going to be known as the sad sack with a dying wife. Over the years we had many such moments—moments where the universe became silently organized in the mirror of her eyes, like a pond at sunrise, and I could see myself plainly, and I could understand that my time on this earth has been nothing more than an elaborate attempt to hide the truth from myself.

Helen and I minded our own business for the next several hours while I thought about my life. In that period of time I came to a conclusion as to why a person could hate this woman, my wife. The fact of her existence was terribly inconvenient.

Over the course of the rest of the morning, I had remained quiet. But in the car on the way to the colonoscopy, I said to Helen, "You're awful quiet."

"I'm all emptied out," she said, and it took me my usual interval to realize she had made another joke, and that I had a decision to make about what kind of a man I was going to be for the duration of all this.

"Well I'm full of enough shit for the both of us," I said.

We were quiet later that day, too, back at home after the colonoscopy, but it was a different version of quiet because by then we had a pretty good idea of the situation. "Are we supposed to speak in a situation like this?" I asked.

"I think I'm just too tired."

"Well then go to sleep."

"I'm scared for you, Bubba."

"Don't—"

"Bubba, I'm going to die."

"C'mon, now, woman."

"Tell me it's okay if I die."

"It's okay if you die."

"Thank you. You're a nice man, you know that? I'm proud of you, Bubba."

Instead of crying, which was one very serious option, I decided I would go sit on the couch and pray. But it didn't work very well, so instead of praying (and instead of crying) a resolution occurred in my brain to write this ridiculous story. What exactly compelled me, I do not know.

Melinda swung by our apartment that evening on her way down to the Sad Kitchen. She softly knocked and I stepped outside and shut the door and we softly talked.

"Hello, Bubba. Is she okay?"

"She's asleep," I said, unsure whether this was true. "I don't think we will make it to the Sad Kitchen tonight. You'll have to make the tickets up yourself and forge her signature. I hereby give you permission. But no funny business, girly."

"Is there anything I can do for you?"

"Yes. Talk to me like a fellow who isn't just a total sad sack."

"Are you capable of cooking your own dinner without causing a toxic explosion?"

"Thank you. What else do you have?"

"Well I guess you could always make yourself a cup of that mud that you call 'coffee'."

"What, you don't like my coffee?"

"I'm sorry, Bubba. I like your coffee just fine."

"Hey!"

"Your coffee is mud!"

"That's better. Now you get out of here. Listen, I've decided to write a story."

"Send my condolences to literature," said Melinda. "What is it going to be about?"

"Just this. Just my wife. Just how she's an angel. Folks need to know that people like her actually *do* exist, as inconvenient as that may be."

141

Melinda made a soft face.

"What's that face?" I said.

"Nothing. If I don't have anything snarky to say, well then I just won't say anything at all."

"You get out of here. Just try not to burn that place down this evening."

That night, as I was settling into bed next to my emptied-out wife, she shifted and then murmured. "Hello, Bubba."

"Shhh," I whispered, "Go back to sleep. Melinda stopped by. Go back to sleep."

"What did she say?"

"The Sad Kitchen is in good hands for the night. Go back to sleep."

"She's a good kid."

"Go back to sleep," I whispered. "You need your rest. Listen, since I can't get any decent prayer going, I've decided to write a story as a replacement for prayer. I shouldn't be talking. You should be sleeping. Go to sleep. I'm sorry. But listen, this story will be a lot like prayer, but a little different, though. It's going to be about the Sad Kitchen. But it's also going to be about you. You're my wife and you're going to be the center of this story."

My wife was quiet for a long time, and I assumed she was asleep. *I'll just have to tell her in the morning,* I thought. *I'll just have to get her permission in the morning.* But the rosy scent that usually accompanies her sleep was not there and soon she murmured, "Okay, but you had better leave out this next part. I would hate to get your story all bloody and messy. Yes, Bubba, you had better leave out this next part."

Next Part:

So that's why I must be very careful here. Strictly speaking, I do not have permission to include this next part. It is unlikely that my wife would haunt me from the grave (being the sweetheart that she is) but she could resort to some cruel practical jokes.

Suffice it to say that this part of the story has been dipped in my wife's blood and smeared with plenty of her guts, and I'd like to wash my hands of it.

Sometimes these days my wife would be in the bedroom and I would be at the kitchen table writing this ridiculous story and she'd say, "Bubba!...Hey, Bubba!"—very urgent.

I would scurry in there to find her reclined in bed yet obviously restless and in a tizzy. "What is it?"

"Don't stop going to mass, okay Bubba?" she would say.

Or, "If you ever find yourself missing me just go ahead and say some prayers to Our Lady, okay Bubba?"

Or, "That Melinda is a good kid, okay Bubba?"

"For God's sake, I know she is. Is that what you called me in here for?"

"Bubba, I'm going to die."

"No you're not. You're alright."

"This wouldn't bother me one bit if I knew it weren't going to be such a hassle for you. You'll be okay when I'm gone, right, Bubba?"

"You're not going anywhere, woman. Quit it."

"How's your story coming?"

"It's getting further and further from childhood."

"Well, don't put this part in there."

"I won't."

She missed the Sad Kitchen. But we were no longer nocturnal critters, and it was not easy to visit a venue that is only open in the nighttime. Sure, Helen wanted to visit, but she was torn because she did NOT want to trouble folks, especially Jack.

"Bubba, don't tell Jack."

"Don't you think Melinda has already told him?"

"Melinda is a good kid."

"I know she is, damn it."

"I'm looking forward to seeing my little boy. That's one good thing about all this—I'll get to see him very soon now. Any day now. I'll bet he's as big as you are, Bubba."

This was how our conversations went—very scatterbrained. It got so that the things she said next had very little relation to what she had said before. "How's your story coming, Bubba?"

"Vern is in some hot water in my story. The 11 o'clock news is about to come on."

"How is old Vern doing?"

"In my story, you mean?"

"No!" she was suddenly excited.

"We haven't seen old Vern in months. You know that, you crazy old woman."

"Vern is a good man, Bubba."

With the mention of Vern's name, a fear which had been, until that day, quite unformulated for many months, finally hardened in my hard, hard head. Vern was dead, I feared, and his cause of death was suicide, I feared.

I went and sat in front of this story and thought about my life. I knew in my soul that the Sad Kitchen was a friendly place. Was that enough to change the fact that Vern was probably a dead man? I was suddenly assailed by visions of the unifying grace of the Sad Kitchen and I had no choice but to say: *Melinda is going to go find Izzy and doggone it I'm going to take it upon myself to go find Vern and bring him home! It's all going to work out! It just has to! The end of my wife's story is at stake here!*

It was nothing but a moment of weakness. I had a sick wife in the other room. It was sentimental and stupid of me, and I think I realized it even while it was happening, but I let my irrationality fuel me:

"Hey lady," I peeked my head into the bedroom and said to my wife, whose eyes were closed but who wasn't asleep because I couldn't smell roses. "I am going to step out for a little bit. Is there anything I should bring home with me?"

"One hot fudge sundae."

"Listen, Helen, whatever happened to the little girl, Izzy? Melinda was going to try to track her down very delicately."

"Izzy?"

"Yes, Izzy. Vern's…You know. *Izzy*. Are you just completely bat-brained? Sorry I don't mean that. *Izzy!* Remember, Melinda was going to track her down very delicately?"

"Melinda is a good kid."

"Listen, I'll be back later this evening with one hot fudge sundae."

"Bubba, I'm going to die soon."

"Oh, for God's sake. You're alright, you crazy woman. You just need a good hot fudge sundae."

"Mmmmmmmm," she said and cozied into a rosy-scented slumber.

I drove downtown. It was daytime. In the hollow parking garage, I shut the door on my automobile, and then it echoed several times overhead like the doors of phantom automobiles.

Here I was, downtown in the daytime. I walked the streets for a while. It was spring, but the day was raw and very gray. The sky was the same color as the concrete all around me. My hands scurried into my jacket pockets like scared little ground animals. The wind was sharp and mean.

I apologize for bringing about this cold and stinging wind, but you must try to feel it on your cheeks while you still can—because in a moment, things will turn quite odd and you will miss being able to decipher where your face stops and everything else begins.

Here we are, folks. Right through here. Some bells clanked against the glass pane of the door and all of a sudden I was inside.

I am being coy, I apologize: the place I entered was the artist's gallery. It was musty and cluttered and the lights were off. Everything was suspended in a state of either repair or disrepair—plenty of stuff covered with blankets and a scattering of cardboard boxes.

The silence of the choking air was such that I was compelled to clear my throat. When I did that, there came a rustling sound like a rat eating a dirty magazine.

Then there came some footfalls on a staircase which I could not locate—it was either underneath me or overhead or inside of me or back in the parking garage. The footfalls were wooden-sounding, and they were hammering me into a petrified state, closing my ribs tighter about my lungs. Breathing was a waste of effort anyway, so musty was this place.

The footfalls were getting closer and closer and were sounding more and more like the return of the echo of my car door back in the parking garage. Then they were done, and I was suddenly face-to-face with the side of a face. Let me try to explain. A human figure was standing with its hands in its pant-pockets and its feet and chest and shoulders and neck square to all these same things of mine, which were also square, but this human figure was wearing a mask that caused its face to appear to be peering directly to the left. There was only one slot for an eye. The other eye must have been covered. Stated simply, it was the mask of a face in profile, if that makes any sense. But if it does make sense, then I'm not explaining it correctly, because really it didn't make any sense at all.

The face in profile was not the face of a human or a horse or a rooster, but it was not NOT any of those things either.

"Hey, Bubba," came a sound in the voice of the artist.

It took me a long time to answer because, first, I had to remind myself what *sound* was, and then what *words* were, and then what *Bubba* was. "Hello," I said like an idiot.

"You can't tell, but I'm smiling right now," said the artist. "I'm delighted to see you."

"I'm smiling too," I said automatically, even though I wasn't smiling, which he could plainly see since I wasn't wearing a mask. This sunk me more deeply into my idiocy. I had to clear my throat again. "That's a mighty nice mask you've got."

"I wear this mask when I meditate."

"That's very nice. Say, why is all your stuff covered with blankets?"

"I'm in a transitory state, you see. I've begun a regimen that requires me to wear this mask for twelve hours per day."

"I guess I caught you at the right time then," I said meaninglessly.

"Or the wrong time," said the artist, and then laughed. His laughter, which seemed to come from out of nowhere (I'm speaking in respect to both time and space, now), unraveled me at my joints and left me floating. I was all disoriented. I was on the other side of the strangest mask I'd ever seen and the cold wind outside the door would have been like the warmest cup of the saddest coffee at that moment. At home my wife would be asleep and giving off her rosy wafts.

I cleared my throat once again. "Listen, I just came by to ask whether you've heard from old Vern. I haven't seen him since the night of…I haven't seen him for a damn long time and I worry about him. He hasn't been at the Sad Kitchen. But you and he have that book together and, well, I thought maybe the business side of that arrangement might have brought the two of you into contact from time to time. Listen, have you heard from old Vern? I worry about the poor guy."

"Come here, Bubba," said the artist. "I would like to show you something. I haven't shown it to anybody else, but I would like to show it to you. You are my man."

"What is it?" I said, but the artist was already leading me somewhere.

I followed. Down a wooden staircase we

went, and then through a hallway into a cellar.

"You are in the bowels of the city right now," said the artist. "Welcome."

There was a torch burning on either side of the hallway—no light other. *You are here*, I told myself and touched my face just to verify that it was still there.

"Right this way. Sorry if this is a little creepy. It's perfectly safe, I assure you. I've had it fumigated and I've verified the integrity of the walling."

"I was just hoping to ask you about old Vern…"

"Right in here, see?" said the artist.

We turned a corner in the cellar and came to a small room that was barred off. It looked just exactly like a prison cell.

"What is it?" I said.

"It's a prison cell."

"Oh."

"It's a product of my own devising. What do you think?"

"I like what you've done with the place."

"Thank you, Bubba. I knew you would understand. I've been wanting to show it to someone, but I thought nobody would care. Then you came strolling in here today and I said to myself, 'This is a sign. If there is one person who will care, it's old Bubba.' Seeing as how you had such a good rapport with old Vern."

"*Had?*" I said, trying to maintain my composure in this strange place. "Listen, do you know anything of Vern's whereabouts?"

"This is where I spend my time nowadays. Do you know why? I like to visualize a tree growing up through the prison cell of my own life."

"Like Vern's did."

"I have contemplated it at great length, and I've determined that Vern is the truest artist I've ever met. Before I met Vern, I believed that art was a way of presenting myself to the world. A form of self-expression. But with Vern's help I've come to a realization: it is the opposite. True art lets the world be expressed through the artist, let's the world pass through the artist until the artist is nothing but expression itself. Yes, Vern understood what it means to take part in creation—like a tree. Do I believe that a tree actually grew up through the floor of Vern's prison cell the way he always claimed one did? No! I have decided that it is an elaborate metaphor on Vern's part for something that seems simple but is actually impossibly complicated, and I am going to figure it out. I'll never try my hand at art again until I've learned what Vern already understood, until I've meditated for many hours—hundreds perhaps!—upon my own prison cell, upon my own tree. Do you see? What do you think, Bubba?"

"I think it's interesting."

"You don't understand."

"I don't have to understand to think it's interesting."

"You think it's stupid."

"Listen, have you seen Vern?"

"FORGET VERN!"

It echoed like the parking garage, but downward. "My wife is sick. Helen is home in bed."

"You better be going."

"I think I better be on my way."

"I agree. Go. GO!"

As I scurried down the hallway, I heard the bars clank shut on the prison cell.

CHAPTER SEVEN

Let me pretend she was dead when I got home. Pretend I was holding the ice cream sundae that I had promised her in one hand and putting the back of my other hand on her cheek, and it was a tragic but peaceful moment filled with the smell of roses.

That's not how it was, of course. I was so stupefied by the artist's strangeness that day that I didn't even remember the sundae, and my wife lived another four weeks, the middle two of which were horrible. The middle two weeks were the period she would have especially wanted me to skip here. By the end of the third week, Melinda had convinced me to call hospice, and they induced peace in our home. "She's sleeping," the hospice folks were obsessed with saying whenever I poked my head in.

"No, she's not," I always replied because I couldn't smell roses. But they never asked me to explain what I meant by that.

My last words to Helen were, "You'll be alright." She died in bed in the summertime with the window open. I was in the other room.

After the burial, Vern was there. The burial ceremony ended with Helen dead in the ground next to her son, the shortstop, and I looked up and, sure enough—it was Vern. He was standing next to Jack in the road that went through the cemetery. When we saw each other, we didn't know whether to shake hands or hug. We decided to shake hands.

"Do you want to get some coffee some evening?" said Vern

"I'm not nocturnal anymore," I told him. "Let's do some morning how about?"

We planned to have some breakfast a few days later.

Melinda kept coming over to check on me in the days after my wife's death. She was wonderful. She had begun to call me "big dog," which I got a kick out of. "Hey big dog." "Doing okay, big dog?" "If you ever want to come back to the Sad Kitchen, we've got a place for you, big dog."

"That nocturnal business isn't for me any longer. I like the sunshine. It does me some good."

"Okay but I need one thing from you. Can you make the tickets?"

"You want me to make the tickets?"

"You can make them up during the daytime and I'll come pick them up from you."

"Maybe in a few weeks," I told her. "I want to finish this damn story about my wife."

"What's happening right now?"

"You're pestering me."

"I mean in the story, you goon."

"You're pestering me in the story, too! Get out of here girly! I'm just fine."

Vern and I met for breakfast on a Wednesday morning as we had arranged on the grounds of the cemetery. Vern looked uncomfortable and shy when he got in the booth and I thought for certain I would have to say the first words, but all of a sudden he said, "So old Bubba is no longer a nocturnal critter."

It was a wonderful icebreaker.

"I had forgotten that the sun existed there for a few years. Where have you been, Vern?"

"Oh, around."

"I was afraid you might have killed yourself, bud."

"Thought about it. Oh man did I think about it. I was going to hang myself from a tree. I thought it would be poetical, at least."

We had some coffee and I had hot cakes and bacon and Vern had eggs and bacon.

I spent a lot of time debating whether to end my wife's story right here while Vern and I are eating breakfast together in the morningtime. But I've decided to include one more note.

The main thing I want folks to understand is that I would have told this story just the same without this next part ever having happened. It is an important story without this next part, because my wife is a good person, and people like her actually *do* exist: that's the main thing I want folks to be able to believe in. This next part isn't important—nobody needs to believe it if he doesn't want to. For all anyone knows, I made this next part up. After breakfast, Vern pulled a sheet of paper out of the breast pocket of his shirt and unfolded it and slid it across the table at me. It was a letter with the most awful handwriting.

Dear Mr. Vern,

I reelly like Timeout For Vernon. Expecley the dove. He was so nice to the bunne. I am in 2nd grade now. My name is Boone. My mom says hi. She helpd me write this but only some words. Her name is Izzy and she says she forgives you. We pray for you every nite so you are lovd. Sorry if nobody loves you. We love you.

      Love
      Boone

Acknowledgements

I would like to thank my parents for their unrelenting love and self-sacrifice and for their support of this book. I would also like to thank my wife for taking it seriously when she could have been off saving lives. Then, of course, there are all the friends in Bowling Green who said this story was worthwhile. Finally, I would like to thank Lauren at Galaxy Galloper Press for all her hard work and reassurance and for reminding us what it means to be a literary citizen.